Ordinary Angels

Ordinary Angels

BRIDGET BIRDSALL

Book design by Flying Pig Productions.
Cover design by Kimberly Puetz.
Cover images from istockphoto.com.

www.bridgetbirdsall.com

ISBN 978-1453850503

For L.P.

Acknowledgments

I AM deeply grateful to my friends and fellow writers at Vermont College for their unwavering encouragement and support, especially my mentors Liza Ketchum, Marion Dane Bauer, Tim Wynn-Jones, and Alison McGhee. I want to extend a special thank you to Lynn Hazen who introduced to me Lissa McLaughlin, who was instrumental in editing this manuscript, and my former high school classmate Kristin Jacobson, who graciously offered her copyediting skills in exchange for art.

My writing would not be possible without my favorite fellow writers, both local and national, who provide inspiration and critical feedback. They include groundbreaking author Nancy Garden and Wisconsin's own Jane Hamilton, Kevin Henkes, and David Rhodes. Moreover, I could not have completed this novel without the audacious women of AROHO, amazing women writers who constantly remind me that words matter.

I am indebted to my key readers and listeners, Pamela Johnson, Ann Angel, Robbie Haroldson, Susa Silvermarie and Kelly O'Ferrell, as well as the entire gang from the FSC who came to cheer me on the first time I read from this book publicly, especially my dear friend Bonnie Brink who helped make it financially feasible to publish this book. I also want to thank the Terry Family Foundation for a Resident Fellowship and a fabulous place to write.

And my family, my sister Kathy who reminds me when I forget that love is always evident. And my son Quinn, who encouraged me to publish a book before I "run out of time." My partner, Roseann, who makes me laugh, who gently pushes me to be all I can be, and who helped birth the character, May, into my first published short story, *Miracle on Monkey Mountain*. And all the people too numerous to name who have in one way or another assured me that this book helped them heal.

People will see what they want. It's only the ones inside who know the truth.

—Anna Quindlen, *Rise and Shine*

CHAPTER 1

The Valley

MOTHER IS raging inside the house.

Outside, you spit a stale piece of Bazooka Joe bubble gum through the diamond-shaped hole in the wire fence that separates your backyard from the brewery. Less than ten feet away a forklift hums and moves about like a giant prehistoric insect, sorting and stacking endless rows of yeasty silver kegs. Someone, somewhere, is roasting Polish sausage with sauerkraut. The sweetness of the meat mixes with the bitter scent of blood from the slaughterhouse where your dad is at work only a few blocks away.

People call this place Pig Valley. At school, kids ask how you can stand to live so close to the smell of all that death. You never know what to say. This is all you've ever known.

"May!"

Instinctively, you run toward Mother's call. From the landing on the back porch she shoves baby Hal's wiggling, wailing body into your arms.

1

"Get him out of my sight," she hisses.

You clasp the back of Hal's emerald green overalls and quickly descend the steps, struggling to hold onto his bucking two-year-old body.

"Shut him up," she adds, "or you'll both wish you were never born."

The screen door slams shut.

She is gone.

Hal's cries ramp up into a high-pitched howl. His small fists flail perilously close to your face. You tighten your grip on the back of his green overalls, grateful for the handle the thick cotton provides. The emerald green corduroy matches his eyes.

You, Hal, and Mother are the only ones in the family who have green eyes. But there is no time to ponder this now. You've gotten into enough trouble at school for *pondering*. Sister Francis says you must get your head out of the clouds. She told your parents that you must learn to focus, or you would have to do sixth grade twice. You definitely do not want to end up in Sister Francis' class again. So you've been trying not to ponder a single thing.

You lug Hal to a red wagon at the edge of the driveway. He wants to run, but you won't let him. The trucks that come up and down Point Road would crush him like a stone. You are the oldest. It is your job to keep him safe. So you hang on tight.

"Shushhh." Your sister, Helen, plops down in the wagon and puts her finger to her lips. Everyone calls you and Helen Irish twins because she was born only eleven months after you were, but you are still a year ahead of her in school.

Together, you try to calm baby Hal, to warn him that if he makes too much noise, Mother will get madder. Then she will beat him with a wooden spoon and it will break across his back and then—he will really, really, really be sorry he was ever born.

But Hal keeps crying. He cries until he can't catch his breath and you're not sure what to do, and you say a secret prayer that he will get tired, which sometimes happens.

"I can't listen anymore." Helen covers her ears. She heads for the swing set where Jacob, who is only six, is pumping so high his toes knock the top of the barbed wire fence. Twank. Twank. Twank.

Helen settles herself on a swing, still holding her hands over her ears. The forklift spits and sputters up and down the bed of an idling delivery truck.

"Not so high," you holler at Jacob over the sound of the coughing machines. This startles baby Hal, who stops crying, gulps in a breath, and stares up at you as if he is trying to figure out who you are.

You smile. Green eyes meet green eyes. There is no mistaking you are brother and sister.

"It's okay," you whisper and brush your lips against his damp forehead.

He stops struggling. His body softens and you turn him over and tuck him under one arm. Then you lean back into the wagon to keep an eye on Helen and Jacob. This is your job. You are the oldest. Dad is counting on you.

Helen unplugs her ears and settles herself on a swing.

The kegs clank and rattle as the forklift swivels around for another load. Usually Hal likes to watch the forklifts, but today he only glances momentarily, then his eyes return to meet yours. He studies you as if he is much older, as if he needs to tell you something, something important, but he's waiting for just the right time.

He reaches his small hand up and touches your cheek.

Your cheek is wet.

How did your cheek get wet?

You never cry. You loosen your grip and use your sweatshirt sleeve to wipe Hal's face, then your own, then you open his tiny fist and kiss the inside of his grimy sweaty palm. He watches as you run your index finger down his lifeline. Aunt Emma taught you how to read palms. But you can't remember what it means if a lifeline is broken, so you make up a fortune. "You will live to be 99 like Grandpa JJ, and have 10 children like Grandmother Golding, and grow big muscles like Dad, and work at Titus Tannery."

Hal watches you carefully. He probably doesn't remember Grandpa JJ, because Grandpa JJ died the same day they shot President Kennedy, just before Hal was born. There is something in Hal's deep green eyes that makes you sad. It seems as if he is trying to memorize your face, as if he is a famous painter and he has to stare and stare and stare to get it just right.

"What?" you ask, knowing he can't answer.

He smiles.

"What?" This time you jiggle him playfully in your arms. A sigh erupts from his small body, then a hiccup, and finally a giggle as he closes his eyes and rests his head against your chest. His blotchy red cheek feels hot against your heart. The front of your red sweatshirt is dotted with dark spots from his tears. His chest begins to rise and fall in rhythm with your own. You smell baby shampoo mixed with his baby sweat and you say a secret prayer that soon he will be able to listen and to understand that he must not cry, he must not get Mother mad.

You lean your cheek against Hal's to give the prayer time to soak in. On the other side of the fence the brewery whistle blows and the forklift stops moving, and all you can hear is the squeak of the swing where Helen and Jacob are having a silent pumping contest and the soft sound of Hal's breathing.

Inside the house even Mother is quiet.

You think how proud your dad will be when he gets home. How he will hug you with his strong muscle arms and toss you in the air and say, "Who's my girl? Who's my best helper?"

Then you think that maybe, just maybe, everything really will be okay. What you don't know—in this moment—is that this will be the only memory you will have of Hal, while he is still alive.

CHAPTER 2

The Accident

"SOMETHING HAPPENED to Hal!" Aunt Emma hollers from the back porch. "May, take Helen and Jacob and go home, right now!"

You dropkick an orange basketball onto the grass and look up to see Aunt Emma motioning frantically with a damp dishtowel. "Go, honey, go, go."

The black telephone receiver is pressed between her shoulder and her ear.

Deep down you know something is terribly wrong. You can feel it.

"What happened?" you shout across the yard.

Aunt Emma doesn't answer. She turns away and says, "Yes... yes... they are on their way..." into the telephone.

Something happened? To Hal? All morning there's been a buzzing in your head and humming in your bones. All morning you could feel it building, like static electricity.

As you run toward Helen and Jacob, you remember how Mother didn't get out of bed again this morning. How her eyes were puffy when you brought in her coffee.

Puffy eyes are not a good sign.

Hal had cried and banged his crib against the wall again until Dad got angry and yelled for you to bring Hal his bottle, but when you did, Hal didn't want it. In fact, he threw it against the wall. You tried, but you could not keep Hal from crying, so you got him out of the crib and brought him into your bedroom where Helen and Jacob were playing Lincoln Logs on the braided rug, waiting to go to church.

Hal must have wanted to be out of his crib. He stopped crying, and after awhile, he let you feed him Cheerios from a pink plastic cup. Then, even when all four of you were ready to go to church, you didn't go, because Dad told Mother he wanted to watch the Packers instead.

This made Mother mad.

Not going to church on Sunday is a sin.

Mother jumped out of bed and stormed into the hallway. She beat Dad's chest with her fists. He yelled at her to calm down, but this made her madder. Then the neighbors upstairs banged on the floor, and Helen plugged her ears and hid under the bed, and Jacob just sang some marching song he made up, still playing Lincoln Logs like he couldn't even hear them. Then, somehow, unbelievably, in the middle of it all, Hal fell asleep in your arms, so you laid him out on the braided rug and covered him with his blue blanket.

From under the bed, Helen suggested you close the door so Hal wouldn't wake up, but Dad came in and said, "May, take Helen and Jacob over to Aunt Emma's house."

Behind him, Mother screamed, "Get them out of my sight."

Something crashed in the hallway.

Dad turned around and said in a loud whisper, "Calm down, for God's sake!"

"What about Hal?" you said.

"Jesus H. Christ," he said under his breath and looked down at Hal. "Let him sleep."

"What about church?"

"We're skipping church. Now, go. Now."

He was starting to get annoyed with you. He depends on you when Mother goes crazy, and even though you'd wanted to go to your cousin's house, you didn't like the idea of leaving Hal all alone. So after Dad left, you kneeled down beside Hal and said a quick prayer that he would stay asleep until you got back and that God would forgive your family for missing church.

You shouldn't have listened to Dad.

Now your feet feel frozen. A cave is hollowing out in your belly and you can't help but think about what happened after you left. When Hal woke up and you weren't there.

You weren't there to make sure he didn't try to run away, to tell him everything would be okay. Now, because you listened to Dad and your family skipped church, which is a definite sin—everything is not going to be okay.

Aunt Emma steps out onto her back porch again. This time the phone is gone and she is wiping her eyes with the red-striped dishtowel.

"May, hurry, honey. Hurry."

She's been crying.

You force your feet to move. You must help Helen and Jacob cross the street. This is your job, you are the oldest, and you know that Dad depends on you.

"But I was just starting to have fun," Helen complains as you grab her hand.

"Something happened to Hal," you say gravely.

You reach down to pull Jacob up off the asphalt. His hand is sticky from the popsicle stick he's been using to rearrange anthills.

Jacob is obsessed with two things: ants and armies.

"There is only one queen," he announces as you pull him to his feet. "She is in charge of the workers—"

"Would you please shut up about the ants," Helen begs, but Jacob just keeps chattering on.

"Worker ants are like soldiers." Jacob trails obediently beside you. "Only instead of finding enemies they have to get food… worker ants always line up one by one… they form a food army…."

Helen plugs her ears and moans. Then, ears still plugged, she asks, "What happened to Hal?"

Your stomach feels like it has swallowed a ball of fire and it's burning your belly from the inside out. Your head feels dizzy. Like it does when you know something you don't want to know.

A siren rings through the air and Jacob begins to mimic it—OoooeeeOOOeeeeOOeeee—until Helen thumps him with her fist. Just before you turn the corner Helen stops in her tracks and she stomps her foot. "MAY—I know you know what happened to Hal, so say it!"

Your mouth tastes like tinfoil. Like the time you had your tonsils out and you threw up a pint of blood.

You can't look at her. Somehow you know that you know, though you don't know how you know.

"May... what happened to Hal?"

Helen looks at you. She knows you better than anyone in the entire world. She knows you know things. When you don't answer, she grabs your hand and yanks both you and Jacob around the corner to the edge of Point Road. "Then I'm going to go see, myself..." she starts to say, then all three of you see the ambulance and the police car. They are parked right in front of your house and the red lights are making cherry drop patterns on the shiny black surface of Point Road. The lights are flashing and flashing and flashing, though someone turned the sirens off.

You tighten your grip on Jacob's hand. He's stopped making any sound.

"Hal?" Helen whispers.

You can barely move your head to look both ways. There are too many cars on Point Road and a policeman is directing traffic. Lucky it is Sunday, so there are not any trucks backed up at the brewery gate, but you still can't see clearly what is going on.

"Why is the policeman at our house?" Jacob asks.

11

"Something happened to Hal," Helen whispers as if she's fallen into a trance. "May knows but she won't tell."

"Why won't you tell?" Jacob stares at you.

Helen's hand has gone limp in your own and Jacob's is so sticky, it's like he's glued to your side. You can't tell them what you know because you don't believe it yourself. Then you spot Dad on the other side of Point Road. He's running down the sidewalk toward you.

He runs out onto the road and holds up his arms. The cars stop and you quickly tug Helen and Jacob along to the other side.

As you cross, you see the white collar and shock white hair of Father O'Rourke. He is standing on your front lawn trying to talk to your mother who is crying hysterically and pulling away from him. Mother screams, "Nooooooo!" You have never seen Fr. O'Rourke without his Sunday robes, and he looks so much smaller than at church. Mother collapses onto the grass and he tries to help her up, but she slaps his hands away.

"Noooo, nooo, nooo!"

The cars on Point Road begin to back up. Someone honks as Dad runs back to safety, all out of breath. There are tears in his eyes, and in that moment you know that everything is definitely not going to be okay. Never, ever, ever have you seen your dad cry.

"Hal?" you hear your own voice ring out.

Your father towers over you. He leans over and puts his hands on his knees, like he is going to share a secret, but he doesn't say a thing, just gathers you all into his strong arms and presses your bodies together in a tight hug.

Finally, he says, "There was an accident." He pauses, then he finishes, "Hal is dead."

"D-E-A-D?" Helen spells the word slowly.

You and Helen look at one another. Even though you're a grade ahead of Helen, you can't spell well, but you know exactly what she is spelling, and you can't believe it either.

"God took Hal up to heaven," he says.

"But why?" Jacob asks.

"It was an accident." Dad straightens up. He puts his hand on your shoulder. "May, I need you to take Helen and Jacob to your rooms and wait until I come. Okay?"

"Where is Hal?" Words simply fly from your mouth.

"Noooooooo!" Mother screams louder as one of the ambulance men rushes over to assist Father O'Rourke. Dad glances back apprehensively. You and Helen and Jacob keep watching Dad. He is the one acting out of character, not Mother.

Father O'Rourke says something about time and healing.

"I have to help your mother now," he says, then turns all three of you toward the house and gives you a little push. As his hand makes contact with your back, his thoughts jump into your head, "*Calm her down, there's no telling what she will do.*"

How do Dad's thoughts jump into your head? Sometimes they just do. Now, your head is pounding like a train, and your heart is banging against your ribs so hard it's bruising up your body from the inside out.

"Go to your rooms and wait 'til I come," he says urgently, and he pushes you harder toward the house.

"Is Hal in there?" Jacob points to the ambulance.

You wonder too. A part of you still doesn't believe that Hal is dead, but Dad isn't listening, he keeps pushing you past Mother and Fr. O'Rourke. He pushes you past Mrs. Novak, who is laid on a small patch of grass where Mr. Novak is fanning her with a Sunday paper.

"Is Mrs. Novak dead, too?" Helen asks.

Dad shakes his head. He pushes you past the police car and the ambulance where Hal's baby body might be.

"Is Hal in the ambulance?" You have to know.

"I told you: Hal is in heaven. He is an angel now... now... May... please take care of Helen and Jacob 'til I come."

"I can take care of myself!" Helen cries and she runs up the back porch steps and slams through the screen door into the house.

You peel away your hand and drop Jacob off at the door of the bedroom he shares with Hal. Jacob licks the stickiness from his hand as you wipe your fingers across the bottom of the church dress you are still wearing, even though no one went to church. You both check the crib to make sure Hal is not there. He's not.

"Stay here, 'til Dad comes," you say and close the door.

Jacob immediately resumes his siren sound. From behind the adjoining bedroom wall, Helen yells, "SHUT UP!"

In the bedroom with Helen, you walk solemnly to the window and sit on top of the radiator cover and peer out toward the front of the house, toward Point Road, hoping to get a glimpse of Hal. Red stars from the siren lights flash across the gritty gray siding of the Bolanski's house. A car honks and you hear a police whistle, you press your nose into the screen trying to see. You pound on the screen, and it crashes to the ground below.

"You're going to be in trouble," Helen warns.

You turn around. She's peeking out from beneath the bed.

"Maybe he isn't really dead," you suggest.

She closes her eyes.

You don't want to say what you usually say. It's a lie. You shouldn't have listened to Dad. You should have known better, but you just left him, and now Hal is dead because of you.

CHAPTER 3

The Question

FOR A long, long time, no one comes to check on you. So you stay in the bedroom and wait for Dad. You wait so long Helen falls asleep. Then, just before it starts to get dark outside, Mrs. Bolanski, who works third shift at the brewery, comes out in her housecoat and slippers. Her red hair is twisted up in pink spongy curlers. You watch as she rubs her eyes and peers down the driveway. She spots you sitting on the windowsill and plucks the neon orange earplugs from her ears.

"Heaven's name, May, what is going on? It looks like the Fourth of July out there." She glances at the screen lying on the ground below the window and then squints up at the flashing lights.

"Hal is dead," you say from your perch, as if you are reporting the weather.

"No!" she gasps. "Dead?" she repeats, and you want to spell it for her like Helen, but you don't know how. A hand flies up to her mouth. "Oh, sweet Jesus," she whispers, and you see the fear flash across her eyes.

"There was an accident," you say.

"What happened?"

You shrug.

You wish you knew.

She turns and trots down her driveway toward Point Road. At that moment a Channel 4 News van pulls up and a man with a camera jumps out to speak with her. Mrs. Bolanski begins to talk with the cameraman and a policeman at the same time. She gestures wildly with her hands. The orange earplugs bob up and down in her thick pale fingers. She seems to be saying a lot, considering she slept through the whole thing.

You watch and try to listen, but all you hear is the hum of the traffic and the wind whipping between the houses, making the swing set squeak even though no one is there to play on it. Today, the wind blows off the lake and the smell of Ambrosia Chocolate overpowers even the yeasty smell of hops and barley from the brewery.

Most people think that Pig Valley smells bad, but when they come to visit and the wind is blowing in off the lake and they smell the chocolate, they usually change their minds.

"I'm getting cold," Helen complains from inside the Snoopy comforter. She keeps it stashed under the bed.

She must have been pretending to sleep. You take one last long sniff of the hot cocoa air and shut the window. The goose bumps on your arms probably mean you are getting cold, too. But you don't feel anything.

"I'm hungry," Helen says.

You walk to the wall that separates your room from Jacob's. On the other side he is humming a strange song that sounds like a cross between an Indian war dance and the opera Grandpa JJ took you to see one Christmas. Lightly, you rap your knuckles on the wall.

"What?" Jacob stops singing.

"Are Mom and Dad out back?" you whisper into the wall. You hear Jacob's feet pad over to his bedroom window.

He pads over to the wall and whispers back, "Nope," then adds, "maybe they are with Hal somewhere."

"Hal is dead, stupid!" Helen is suddenly standing beside you. She thumps the wall. Helen has no patience for Jacob or his noises or his make-believe worlds.

"You're stupid," Jacob retorts, thumping his side of the wall.

"Don't call him stupid." You grab Helen's arm before it hits the wall again.

Jacob goes back to humming. Helen shakes you loose, "You are not the boss of me!"

A few minutes later, Dad appears at the bedroom door. He's holding Jacob's hand.

"Girls… are you hungry?"

Both you and Helen nod. You want to ask where Hal is. But you don't want to make Dad cry. He gently guides Jacob into the bedroom. Jacob is holding a bucket of chicken, and the smell of the grease tightens around your stomach like a twist tie. Dad hands you a bag of plastic utensils and a huge stack of thin paper napkins.

"Mother is resting. Eat this and play a game or something, okay?"

After Dad closes the door, the three of you sit cross-legged on the floor. You give Jacob the drumsticks because they are his favorite, but there are only two chocolate milks so you stick two straws in yours. That way Jacob can at least taste it even though he has a milk allergy. A little won't hurt him.

Helen is so hungry she puts seven french fries in her mouth at once. Then she almost chokes and she spits the whole mess onto the rag rug. You try to clean it up with a paper napkin but it keeps pilling up and ripping and the grease leaks out all over your hands and then, somehow, gets on your good church dress.

"Mom's gonna be mad," Helen says.

You think about telling her it's her fault. You don't.

After that, even though you are hungry, you can't eat a thing. So you just sit between Helen and Jacob, keeping the peace while you pick all the skin off the chicken thigh in front of you. After you peel all the meat away from the bones, you toss the whole mess back into the bucket, lick your fingers, and drink down what's left of the chocolate milk—way too fast.

The milk immediately begins to slosh around in your stomach.

When Helen and Jacob are done eating you clean up after them, too. Then you pull the Trouble board game out from under the bed. In the middle of the board is a bubble with two dice. You push the bubble to make the dice hop.

Kur—pop.

"I get to go first," Jacob calls.

Trouble is Jacob's favorite game. He pushes the bubble up and down. Kur—pop. Kur—pop. Kur—pop.

Helen's hands fly to her ears. "I hate board games." Helen tries to push the Trouble board back under the bed, but you rescue it.

"I'll only play Candy Land," Helen says.

"How about Trouble first and then Candy Land?" You really don't feel like playing anything. Helen crawls into her bed and you let Jacob beat you two times in a row. Finally, Dad comes in to compliment all of you on how quiet you've been.

He pulls you aside. "May," he whispers, "can you be my helper tonight and switch beds with Jacob, so he won't be afraid?"

"Is Hal's body up in heaven?"

Dad looks like he's going to cry again. But he doesn't.

"They will keep him at the hospital until the funeral."

A million questions jumble around in your brain. You've never been to a funeral.

"Where's Mom?" Helen asks. Jacob looks up from the floor. He is lying on his stomach pretending the board game pieces have come to life. He keeps pushing the bubble over and over again and knocking the pieces over like they are being bombed. Kur—pop—kur—pop—kur—pop—

"Mother's resting," Dad says, reaching down to stop Jacob from pushing on the bubble.

Dad doesn't look at them. He is looking at you, waiting for an answer.

"Sure." You look at Jacob. "I'm not scared."

And it's true. Besides, you know Jacob has wanted to sleep in the top bunk forever.

Jacob is listening and he abandons the game pieces and scrambles up the ladder to check out his new domain. "General George," he announces, "will like it up here."

No one asks who General George is.

"Good girl." Dad pats your back. "I'll go sit with your Mother."

You go to the bathroom but skip brushing your teeth. They can't be too dirty. You hardly ate anything today and you drank the chocolate milk so fast, it probably didn't even touch your teeth.

CHAPTER 4

The Leprechauns

YOU PULL on your favorite frog-print pajamas as Helen barges through the door. "I'm not changing in front of him," she says. She spots your church dress all bunched up in a ball on the radiator. "Better hang that up before you have to sleep in the pee-bed."

You ignore her. Jacob wets his bed almost every night, but you don't care. You want to be in Hal's room and feel close to him. Even if his body is at the hospital.

In the kitchen, you fill a metallic green tumbler full of water then walk through the kitchen to the back bedroom where Jacob and Hal usually sleep. Every sound is amplified: the neighbors' TV playing upstairs, the squeak of your bare feet on the linoleum floor, the whoosh-whoosh-whoosh of the dishwasher Dad has turned on, even though it's practically empty. Every night the dishwasher's white noise blocks out the street sounds. It helps everyone fall asleep.

In the bedroom, Hal's white crib stands empty against the wall.

You close the door behind you and stand in the shadowy street light that pours through the back window. The light illuminates the crib slats against the wall. Hal's powder blue Morgan dog is wrapped up in an old baby blanket as if it's just had a bath. You reach through the crib slats, but a sound halfway between a screech and a howl freezes your hand in midair.

You listen.

Dad's voice is low. He is talking to Mother. You hear a moan, then another screeching sound, and then Mother starts to cry. You wish you were in your own bed so you could hear better, but the whoosh-whoosh-whoosh of the dishwasher blocks what Dad is saying. Silently, you slip your arm out from between the crib slats.

The room smells like a diaper pail and bleach as you peel back Jacob's racing car bedspread and sniff the sheets. They smell more like Pig Valley than pee. Relieved, you crawl in Jacob's bed, pull the sheets up to your chin, and close your eyes, but you feel wide awake. It is your habit to stay awake late into the night, especially when Mother is not asleep yet. But tonight, Mother won't spank Jacob for wetting the bed, or Hal for making noise.

Things are different when Dad is home, because if Mother slams the kitchen drawers searching for wooden spoons, Dad will tell her to calm down.

Tonight, everyone is safe—even Hal. Because he's still at the hospital.

Your mind starts to picture him lying in the hospital and you wonder what would happen if he just woke up, if he just came back to life, like Jesus. This gets you thinking of Jesus and miracles. Why did God take Hal up to heaven in the first place? Why didn't he just take you? Hal had hardly had a chance to live. If God knows everything—he knows you are oldest, he knows you aren't afraid to die, he knows you know how to hurt and how not to cry. Poor Hal, he didn't even know how to be quiet.

You'd have gone.

You roll over on your side and stare at Hal's empty crib. The smell of bleached sheets makes your eyes water, so you think a prayer even though thinking of God makes you mad... *Our Father who art in heaven... hallowed be thy name... thy kingdom come, thy will be done on Earth as it is in—*

The phone rings in the kitchen outside the bedroom door.

Dad clomps out from his and Mother's bedroom. "Hey Jim... no... no... a size two, yes, I think that'll work... the medical examiner... tomorrow... Thursday's fine... thanks."

He clomps into the pantry, where you hear the sound of bottles clank before he goes back to bed.

Hours pass.

You stare at the crib.

Finally, you force yourself to look at the ceiling. Your bones hurt and you are not tired and there is a crucifix hanging over Hal's crib and it makes you sick to look at it and you try not to think about what God let happen to his very own son. Nothing makes sense. Feelings back up in your brain. You have no words for them. You know Jesus had to die for everyone's sins, but you don't think Hal should have had to die, just because God wanted him up in heaven.

Didn't God have enough friends up in heaven already? All of the saints and Grandpa JJ and President Kennedy and the Baily's beagle dog Caesar?

From what you can see Hal is better than God, because he couldn't have even had many sins. He wasn't even old enough to know about sin.

Your chest starts to hurt again. If God is supposed to be in charge and if he is supposed to be so good—why did he let your brother get killed, why did he take him up to heaven without even giving him a fair chance? And why does he let your Mother go crazy? And if he is supposed to be so good, if he is really real, why can't he just make Hal come back like Lazarus? Maybe, just maybe, if he did—you would believe in him.

You'd believe he was really real.

You squeeze your eyes shut determined not to cry. You never cry. You are strong. Dad is depending on you. You are the oldest. But they just come, the tears, they start to squeeze out and you open your eyes to wipe them away and there he is—HAL!

He is breathing.

He is alive!

He stands at the edge of his crib in his blue bunny pajamas and smiles at you.

You blink and he is still there.

You close your eyes and open them again, slowly—and he is *still* there!

You want to shout his name.

Call to him.

To yell—*I knew you weren't dead!* But you can't move. It's as if God has flash-frozen you in place. Hal reaches out his little hand, the ice melts instantly. You throw off Jacob's covers and leap out of Jacob's bed and run to hug him, but when you try to touch him there is nothing there. Only air. You grasp at the air and the room begins to fill with colors. Millions and million of colors like the stained glass windows at church. They begin to spill out and spin around you. Then the colors turn into little leprechauns with wings and they dive and float and make Hal laugh and both of you reach out to try and grab the colors, but like Hal, they too are only air.

You feel the tears running down your cheeks, you are laughing and crying at the same time. You have never seen Hal so happy, and he looks at you with his air-only eyes like he is trying to say everything is going to be okay, but you already know it's not. It's too late—he is dead. However you spell it, he is only air.

Then everything goes black.

When you wake up you are back in Jacob's bed.

Hal is gone.

The leprechauns are gone.

You sit up and look around. Who put you back into Jacob's bed? It's still dark outside, but you remember the colors. You will never forget them. How they lit up the room. How they made Hal laugh.

CHAPTER 5

The Smells

THERE IS an odd sensation in your chest, like an invisible hand is inside of your chest, squeezing your heart and you wonder if maybe your heart has stopped. Like Hal's. Is this what it feels like when your heart stops? But you know if it did stop it must have been only for a minute, because you breathe into the palm of your hand and feel the heat of your own breath and this means you are still alive. Just to make sure, you press your face into Jacob's pillow and suck in the smells of Pig Valley. You can smell them all—the yeast, the hops, the barley, the roasting meat, the bloody hides drying in the mechanical breeze at the slaughterhouse where Dad works, the dog chow and monkey chow and all the different chows they make at the tannery, the chocolate from Ambrosia, even the butter smell of Mrs. Novak's potato pancakes, and only the tiniest, faintest smell of pee.

Yes, you are still alive. Even if you don't want to be.

29

CHAPTER 6

The Novaks

THE NEXT morning Dad comes in with two big empty boxes from Titus Tannery. His eyes look like two slits in his head and his whole face is ruddy red like it gets when he's been out all night playing poker.

"No school today," he says. "Go see your Mother."

He waits for you to get out of Jacob's bed. You wonder if you should tell him about Hal and the leprechauns. You ask, "What are the boxes for?"

"Go see your Mother," he repeats.

You scoot out of bed into the kitchen. He shuts Hal and Jacob's door behind you.

You stand outside the door and listen to his breathing on the other side. Your bare feet stick to the cool linoleum floor. There is a dark spot near your toes and you crouch down to touch it.

"May?"

Mother calls.

Someone has done a bad job cleaning up the spot. It smells like blood.

"Maaay?"

It smells like Dad's shirts from the slaughterhouse, it smells like a bad mosquito bite that's been scratched a million times, it smells like skin and dirt and earth mixed with metal, and it especially smells like the time you chewed Bazooka Joe bubble gum with a split lip.

"MAY!"

You wipe your hand against the leg of your frog pajamas. No time to ponder. Behind Hal's door Dad begins to break apart the crib with his bare hands.

Helen comes running through the kitchen to fetch you. She stops and puts her hands over her ears. "Why aren't you coming? Mom's gonna get mad."

"I am!" you yell.

Helen can't block out the snap, snap, snap. "*What* is Dad doing in there?"

You don't answer, but turn and run to Mother's bedroom. Helen follows, still holding her ears.

Mother is propped up on two pillows. She pulls you in close to her and gives you a hug. Her breath is sour. "It's going to be okay," she says.

Helen and Jacob are still in their pajamas, too. Jacob stands at the edge of the bed with a Cheerio stuck on the side of his face. A white milk mustache trims his upper lip.

"What is Dad doing?" You lean away from her sourness.

"He's putting Hal's things away. May, I want you to take Helen and Jacob over to the Novaks. Tell Mr. Novak we forgive him."

"For what?"

"For killing Hal."

"*Mr. Novak killed Hal?*" You say each syllable slowly, as if the words are a foreign language to your tongue.

"It was an accident," Helen explains, acting like you are younger than her and she has to help you understand. "Hal got run over by the Novak's car." Helen's hair is knotted on the side of her head and she looks like she's been crying. "Hal is an angel now."

"It was an accident," Mother repeats and nods at Helen. Then, she says to all three of you, "Hal is in heaven, it was an accident—now, go get dressed in your Sunday clothes and come back here so I can make sure you're respectable."

"Uhhh—" Jacob starts to protest.

"Go!" There's an undertow in Mother's voice, so you leave her and do as you're told.

The blue church dress with the lace collar is still rumpled up on the radiator. You pull it over your head anyway, and put on your patent leather shoes with two stiff white ankle socks. In the bathroom, you try to comb the tangle out of the back of your hair, but it hurts too much, so you comb your bangs and leave it at that.

Helen loves getting dressed up. She puts on her pink dress that matches yours, but hers is not wrinkled. Somehow, even though she's taken a nap in it, she's managed to keep it smooth.

Jacob appears at your bedroom door in his white shirt and pin-on black bow tie. Dad must have helped him find his clothes. The only sound coming from Jacob's room now is the sound of drawers opening and closing.

"I didn't wet it," Jacob says proudly as he stands in the doorway pointing up at the top bunk.

"Yes, you did," Helen taunts as she pulls on her own patent leather shoes. They are your old ones, which Helen hates, because you managed to get a huge hole in the toe after using them for manual brakes on your banana seat bike. Mother had them patched at the Buster Brown shop, and now, Helen says, it makes the shoes look so ugly, every time she has to wear them she throws up.

Helen does throw up a lot, but you doubt it's the shoes' fault.

"How come it smells like pee in our room?" Helen sniffs the air.

"I didn't pee," Jacob protests.

You step up onto the ladder rung of the bunk bed and pull back the sheets. They're dry. You jump down and give Jacob a high five, and he smiles. You take his hand and lead him back to Mother's bedroom. Helen follows behind you sticking out her tongue at Jacob. You narrow your eyes so she will knock it off.

"I hate this family," she says under her breath.

Mother's eyes are closed. A pillbox and an empty wine glass sit on the bedside table. Piled on the floor beside the bed is the stack of books she reads when she can't sleep.

"Mother?" you say softly.

Her eyes flutter open. Dark craters hang beneath them. She reaches out feebly to straighten Jacob's bow tie.

He flinches. "I didn't pee the bed."

"Good boy," she coos, and strokes his cheek.

Smiling, relieved, he snuggles in close to her, but after a few seconds her eyes close and her hand drops back to the bed.

"She's sleeping," you whisper to Jacob, because you can see he wants Mother to touch him some more. Helen looks at you. Even she feels a little sad for Jacob. Mother's niceness never lasts.

"We better go," you say gently, taking Jacob's hand.

Helen takes his other hand and you both lead him out of the room through the kitchen, down the back porch steps, across the driveway to the Novak's apartment.

The tomatoes along the fence, where Mr. Novak sometimes lets you take turns holding the big silver watering can, have all been picked. In the summertime, Mr. Novak wears a ribbed sleeveless T-shirt and wipes the sweat from his forehead with a blue bandana he keeps stuffed in the back pocket of his brown gardening pants. He has a number tattooed on his wrist from the war. He and Mrs. Novak don't go to church on Sunday. The war made them not believe in God anymore.

Once when Jacob kept asking Mr. Novak about the war, Mr. Novak said it was more important for him to remember to water his tomato plants when they look thirsty. And to love the children in the world, like he does us, than it is to think about war.

Mrs. Novak loves us too, but her English is hard to understand. She always wants to feed us too many potato pancakes.

When you reach the top porch step, you pause. Suddenly, you can't remember why Mother sent you here.

Helen drops Jacob's hand and looks at you with her—
now what—eyes. Jacob stares at the milk jugs lined up on
the windowsill. He's probably hoping they have chocolate
milk inside, which he shouldn't have anyway.

Mr. Novak's car is not parked in the garage. Later, you
learn the police took it to check for Hal's blood. There
wasn't any.

Helen nudges her shoulder against yours. "Knock," is all
she says.

You can hear a television set playing inside. You have
only been inside a couple of times. It is a narrow side-by-
side, stuffed with old-fashioned furniture and pictures of
people from Poland. You peer through the white lace curtains covering the window glass on the back door.

Helen nudges you again. Her eyes say—*are you going to
knock?*

You knock.

Through the lace curtains you see Mrs. Novak making
her way to the door.

"Come in, come in, children, you want maybe, some
potato pancake?"

Helen and Jacob look at you, but you shake your head
no.

Mr. Novak hollers from the living room. "Ida, those children, they don't want to eat, send them here."

Helen and Jacob file behind you into the living room.
Mr. Novak says something in Polish to Mrs. Novak and
she goes over and turns the sound off on the black and
white television set.

"Ida, please, you sit." Mr. Novak is sitting in a big beige easy chair wearing a maroon bathrobe and you can see his ribbed white T-shirt under it. He motions to a floral patterned sofa.

Mrs. Novak says something to him in Polish and he says, "No Ida, no milk, remember, the boy, maybe... crème soda, yes?"

She turns to Jacob. "You want maybe crème soda, yes?"

"Please," Jacob says politely and glances at you to make sure.

"Me, too," Helen adds.

And before Mrs. Novak can even ask, you nod. She disappears back into the kitchen, where you hear the *psssst* from a soda bottle and the clank of ice.

Helen sits down, too. She stares at the television set.

Jacob sinks onto his knees between the sofa and the coffee table, eyeing the bowl of candy in the middle of the coffee table.

Mr. Novak clears his throat.

"Children, the news, you see this morning?"

Helen and Jacob look at you and you shake your head no. "Where's your car?" you ask.

"Police bring it back today."

Helen grabs Jacob's arm as it snakes its way to the candy bowl. "Don't be a pig!"

"Please, have some... children... please... is fine," Mr. Novak offers.

Grabbing a handful, Jacob leaps back up onto the sofa out of Helen's reach. "He said I could!"

Helen sighs, narrows her eyes at you, like you should do something about Jacob, but you're not sure what to do, in fact, you can't even remember why Mother made you come over here in the first place. Something has filled up your brain with black dust and erased all its memories.

Mr. Novak pushes the bowl across the table closer to you and Helen. "Please," he practically begs.

Not wanting to be impolite, you pick a piece from the bowl. The candy looks like a miniature container of Neapolitan ice cream.

Helen doesn't take one. She just looks at her shoes and presses the patched toe into the worn rug. The air in the skinny room presses in on you.

"Maybe... funeral on Friday, no?" Mr. Novak says and picks a piece of candy for himself. There are lots of choices but he picks a Neapolitan, too.

Crinkle. Crinkle. Crinkle. Everyone unwraps theirs at once.

Mrs. Novak comes back into the room with a tray of sodas and hands each of you a glass. The white layer of the Neapolitan candy sticks to your teeth and you try to scrape it off with your tongue, and then the grassy taste of coconut explodes in your mouth and you want to spit it out. Only there's nowhere to spit it except into the soda glass, so you tuck it into the back of your cheek, take a sip of the fizzy soda, and suck on the next layer of chocolate to cover up the taste.

"What's a funeral?" Jacob asks.

You remember watching the funeral on television when President Kennedy got shot. People said it was because he was Irish, but Dad didn't think so. He said they buried his body with all his secrets and that's as it should be, because once someone is dead what's the use of mucking in the past? People need to move on. The country needs to move on.

Mr. Novak takes a sip of his soda. His knotty fingers tremble.

You think of Hal's only-air body floating up to God.

What will happen to Hal's real body after the funeral?

Will it turn into a skeleton?

How long will it take?

Is it already a skeleton?

Is a funeral parlor like a slaughterhouse?

Mr. Novak clears his throat. "Um… a funeral… is like what you call…?" He snaps his fingers and Mrs. Novak jumps in and says something in Polish. Mr. Novak finishes, "…what you call a ceremony. Like for Catholic Mass. The peoples come to share the sadness in their hearts, they learn of love and forgive, yes?"

The lump of coconut moves down into your throat, threatening to cut off your air, as though the word *forgive* has caused the coconut to blow up like a balloon.

You look at Mr. Novak. He did not kill Hal. It is your fault, but you can't say anything, not one word, because the coconut ball, lodged right over your voice box, won't let you speak.

Mrs. Novak suddenly looks like she is going to cry. Her hands fidget in her lap. She has old hands too, paler than Mr. Novak's. Mr. Novak reaches over and puts his hand on hers.

Everyone is quiet again.

Jacob sucks down the remainder of his soda in one long gulp and then lets out a long loud burp. Helen knocks him with her elbow in disgust.

"Don't be such a pig."

Because he lives in Pig Valley, Jacob thinks that "pig" is a compliment. He makes himself burp again. This time even louder, like when he and Uncle Ike try to spell M-i-s-s-i-s-s-i-p-p-i in a single burp.

Mr. Novak's eyes light up and he laughs.

"Ida, he likes soda, maybe you give him more, yes?"

Mrs. Novak stands up ready to make another trip to the kitchen, but just then, Babushka comes cautiously creeping down the steps.

"Look!" Jacob points.

"Ah," Mr. Novak exclaims in surprise. "Babushka, you come to say hello, maybe?"

The overfed orange tabby cat sits down on its back haunches and carefully eyes the odd menagerie of old people and children.

Mr. Novak smiles at Jacob. "Babushka came when he heard you… yes?"

Jacob shrugs and smiles back.

They begin to laugh. Helen looks up at the cat, and she starts to laugh too. Then you and Mrs. Novak join in, and soon everyone is laughing. Laughing and laughing, until laughter rolls through the room like a wave, until you swallow the coconut ball which moves down and tickles the deepest part of your belly and all the while Babushka acts like he doesn't even care, he lifts his back leg and licks and licks and licks, as if none of you are there, as if he's not one bit embarrassed and this makes everyone laugh more. When it is time to leave, you hear Mr. Novak whisper something behind you. "Those children, Ida, ah, I heard nothing with that baby boy, no bump, nothing, but maybe... the police say... maybe when we went to market, maybe we hit the little one... Ida, this kill me... I sell that damn car... I never drive again...."

And he never did.

Six months later, in the exact same spot where Hal's body was found in a pool of blood, Mr. Novak dropped dead in the driveway. They had to pry his fingers loose from the watering can he used for his tomatoes.

CHAPTER 7

The Limo Ride

STANDING ON the porch in the pressed black and purple checked dress Aunt Cleo bought for the funeral, you watch the biggest blackest car you've ever seen creeping down Point Road. It's so long it looks like two cars put together. Cars like this don't usually drive through Pig Valley, so people all up and down Point Road step out onto their porches to stare at it.

Helen, who is standing next to you in an identical dress, only one size smaller, looks up from the chapter book Aunt Cleo gave her and reads the sign on the side of the car, "O'Leary's Funeral Home."

Mr. O'Leary is Dad's best friend.

"He buries people for a living," you explain to Helen. She looks at you like she's known this for about a million years and how smart can you be anyway, because you can barely read.

You hate it when Helen acts smarter than you. You try to ignore her. She turns away and goes back to her reading. You wish she would read out loud so you could hear the story, but Helen doesn't like to read out loud and since you're a grade ahead of her in school, you figure you'd better learn on your own anyway.

The front door opens. Aunt Cleo sends Jacob out onto the porch to join you. He is wearing a new suit, too, and his bow tie matches your dresses.

Jacob is singing some new song he made up and slapping his thighs like an Indian drum.

"Buuum… bum… bum… bum…."

"May, I'll finish up in the kitchen," Aunt Cleo makes a motion with her stumpy arm over Helen and Jacob's heads. "You're in charge out here, understand?" She looks down Point Road at the approaching limo. "When they get here, you wait 'til I come, okay?"

You nod.

Aunt Cleo is your dad's only sister. She lives in California and comes to visit once a year. Her left hand got cut off in an accident at the meat packing plant when she still lived with Grandmother Golding. After the accident, she thought that a place with more sunshine would help her stump heal faster, so she moved. Now, she lives right on the ocean and walks to the beach every day. Sometimes, she even swims with the dolphins. Someday, if Dad lets you, she said you could come out and visit her and swim with the dolphins too.

She sent you a postcard with dolphins on it and you keep it in your secret wish box, which is really one of Grandpa JJ's old cigar boxes.

Dad says he has no interest in going to the land of fruits and nuts, which is what he calls California when Aunt Cleo isn't around.

Helen looks up from her book to watch Jacob, who begins to drum on the porch railing instead of his thighs. "Buuuum, bum, bum, bum, buuuuum, bum, bum, bum…." His song becomes more intense.

Aunt Cleo pats your head with her good hand. "Such a good girl," she says, and then adds for Jacob's benefit, "No monkey business out here. Keep those clothes clean and the racket down," and she bustles back inside.

All week Aunt Cleo has helped to organize the people who come and go. Some you know from Sacred Heart Church, but most of them you don't. The ones from Dad's work all look the same, most of them live in Pig Valley, but you don't know their names, they blur together, men and women with slightly freckled skin, strong shoulders, and bloodstained hands. They speak sparingly and stand on the bottom porch step offering casseroles filled with tuna and noodles, German sausage and sauerkraut, scalloped potatoes and ham, pans of lasagna with homemade sauce, Swedish tea rings, and Polish donuts. Your kitchen is overflowing with uneaten food. It looks like a giant birthday party. Though everyone knows it's not.

At breakfast Helen threw up again. Aunt Cleo admonished all of you for eating too many sweets. "Enough pastries," she said, shaking her stump at you. "Kids need protein." She made omelets with Velveeta cheese and little chunks of ground-up green pepper.

Helen refused to eat hers.

Helen thinks Velveeta cheese is disgusting. She ate Cheerios instead. She used to hate Cheerios too, but now she says everything that was Hal's favorite is hers, too.

You hate it when Helen gets all fussy about things. That's what makes her throw up. If she gets upset, she can practically throw up on command, which means you can never win a fight with her. Mother always blames you for making Helen throw up. And Mother doesn't want to clean up any more messes.

You and Jacob watch as the black limo pulls slowly up in front of the house. It has three doors on the side, and two look like they can open up together like Cinderella's pumpkin carriage. It is stretched out so long it blocks part of the Novaks' driveway.

Past the car, you see the slats from Hal's crib sticking out of one of the green garbage cans alongside the brewery fence. You look over to see if Helen sees, but she is busy reading and Jacob is so mesmerized by the limo, he's leaning over the railing staring at it in awe.

One week ago Hal died.

Inside the house, in Jacob and Hal's room, everything has been rearranged. The crib is gone, all of Hal's clothes and toys are at Goodwill, and all the pictures of Hal have disappeared. Every sign of Hal has been erased. Even his name has become a secret. No one says it out loud.

Neither you, nor Helen, nor Jacob has seen your Mother since the morning she sent you to the Novak's house.

You'd rather not think about that. You're still feeling bad you didn't want Mrs. Novak's potato pancakes, or tell Mr. Novak that your family forgave him, or say anything about it being your fault, because if you'd stayed with Hal, if you hadn't listened to your Dad, things would be different.

A tall dark-skinned man steps from the driver's side of the long black car. He is wearing white gloves and a fancy blue suit with a matching hat.

"This the O'Malley place?" he asks.

Jacob's jaw drops and he whispers, "A… soldier?"

Helen looks up from her book. She rolls her eyes.

"Not a soldier, stupid, a chauffeur."

"This is it," Aunt Cleo calls out, suddenly standing behind you. She waves with her stump from the porch. "We need a few more minutes," she says, and turns to Helen. "Don't call your brother stupid. It's not polite."

You give Helen a look and she sticks her tongue out at you. Aunt Cleo pretends not to see.

The limo man leans against the car and lights a cigarette. The insides of his palms are pink. Did the color of his skin somehow get washed off?

"Do we get to ride with him?" Jacob asks, hanging onto the porch rail, as he bounces up and down and the wooden planks wiggle under your feet.

"As soon as your Mom and Dad are ready," Aunt Cleo says. Then she, too, pulls a cigarette from a beaded pocketbook. She puts it to her lips, fishes out a lighter and lights it up—all with her good hand.

You step away from her smoke to study the uniformed man. You hate smoke because they showed a movie at school about how it can turn your lungs black.

You don't know a single adult who is smart enough not to smoke.

You think about black lungs, and this makes you think about black skin and you wonder why some people have it. There are no black families in Pig Valley, and there are no black kids at Sacred Heart, but you have seen black kids before, down by Jack's Grocery store. And in New Jersey your Grandmother Golding has a black maid named Bell, who taught you how to make homemade Thousand Island dressing out of ketchup, relish, and mayonnaise. It does not make sense to you why some of the people in Pig Valley are afraid of black people, because you aren't. Bell is the nicest grown-up in the entire world. You love how she smells like Dove soap and talcum powder and earth. She calls you and Helen and Jacob, and Hal, when he was alive, her "beautiful chillins." When she gives hugs, she pulls you in tight and whispers in your ear, "Oh, such beautiful chill-ins, um mmm, the Lord done good when he made you all."

Helen loves Bell too. She stops reading her book to look at the dark-skinned man.

"Maybe he's married to Bell," she suggests, and you nod. You don't think so, because Bell lives in New Jersey where Grandmother Golding lives now and that's pretty far away, but you don't want to fight.

Dad steps out onto the front porch with Mother holding onto his arm. Mother is dressed in her church clothes. A dark veil drops down from her hat and covers her eyes.

Jacob forgets about the limo and the chauffeur driver and runs to Mother.

"Mama," he cries, but all Mother does is absently shoo him away like she's a zombie.

"That's enough," Dad says, "Let's get in the car." He motions Jacob towards Aunt Cleo.

Under her veil Mother doesn't make a peep.

All of you make your way down the front porch steps. The limo driver snubs out his cigarette and opens the back doors to a little room with a semicircle of plush red car seats.

"Should we get inside?" you ask when you reach the door.

"Let Mother go first," Dad says, and you step back as Dad and the driver help her. She is walking slowly and seems unsteady on her heels. Maybe it is hard for her to see through the veil. After they have settled her in, Dad crawls in beside her and then, one at a time, Aunt Cleo shuffles the rest of us through the door, then she climbs in last.

The chauffeur closes the door behind her. He stares at her stump.

In your head you hear him wondering how it happened.

Mother sits by the window not looking at anyone. As the limo begins to move she is so still, it's as if she's fallen asleep sitting up.

After opening and closing all of the little compartments, Jacob squeezes himself between Dad and Mother by kneeling on the floor and putting his head in Mother's lap. This time, she doesn't pat his head or even acknowledge him. She just keeps staring out the window. Like a mannequin. Like she's not even real.

You reach over and rest a hand on Jacob's shoulder and he turns and puts his head in your lap instead, so you lean down and snuggle him. Yesterday was his birthday. No one mentioned it, and you wonder if he forgot. You think that maybe after the funeral you should have a party for Jacob with a cake and seven candles, because after soldiers and ants, Jacob's favorite thing in the entire world is cake, especially Great Grandma Meadow's Irish caramel cake.

The limo hits a bump and both of you fly up in the air for a second. His head lands back in your lap and he giggles. This makes you giggle, too, and he looks up at you and you smile and comb your fingers through his thick blond hair.

"Shhhh," you whisper, because the limo feels like church.

Now that he is seven, you say a special prayer that he will not wet the bed anymore.

Mother says he's way to old to be wetting his bed and you know it's true, but the week before Hal died, Jacob wet his bed and you heard Mother tell Dad he did it on purpose. That night Dad came home early from work and made her stop hitting Jacob, because she hit him so hard his nose started to bleed and it splattered all over the walls and the blanket. Dad told you to clean it up and change Jacob's sheets so he could calm Mother down. Jacob's sheets got tangled, and then the material ripped and Mother saw it happen, and she would have come after you too, but Dad held her back.

She kept yelling that she had enough goddamn work on her hands. Now, Aunt Cleo's doing all of the laundry, so you don't have to worry about it. Aunt Cleo says she likes helping out and she is very good at it too. She can fold towels twice as fast as you, and she uses her chin to hold things. She calls her chin her pincher, and she uses it like a third arm. Aunt Cleo says a person never knows how strong they are 'til they've been tested.

The limo has dark-tinted windows. How is it possible to see the houses and cars going by on the outside if no one can see you inside? The limo pulls up in front of O'Leary's Funeral Home and the driver hops out and comes around to open the back doors.

"Here you go, Sir." He tips his hat after he helps your dad get Mother out. Aunt Cleo opens the door on the other side and hops out on her own. Jacob leaps to his feet. He can stand up inside the car and he jumps down to follow Aunt Cleo.

You and Helen are the last to get out and the driver offers you a hand. He has kind eyes, but he is still a stranger, so you jump down on your own, but Helen puts her hand in his. He says to her, "There yah go, Miss."

Everyone heads up the marble steps to the funeral home, except Helen. She's still holding onto the driver's hand. You grab her elbow and try to make her follow, but she shrugs you away.

"I hate this family," she whispers, and you are not sure what to do, because the man's eyes open wide, but he doesn't say anything.

Helen looks up at him. "Will you marry me?"

"Oh, missy," he smiles and somehow manages to loosen her grip. He says with a laugh, "That's a mighty compliment."

You grab Helen's hand and drag her up the steps to the door. She keeps looking back and smiling at the man, who tips his hat to her. This is the most you can ever remember Helen smiling.

"He was nice," Helen says in a sing-song voice as the funeral home door shuts heavily behind you.

"He'll be an old man when you grow up."

"I know," she says, dreamily, "but he'll still love me, I can tell."

Your ears begin to buzz as this scene starts playing itself over and over in your head.

CHAPTER 8

The Funeral

EVEN though your dad and Mr. O'Leary are best friends, you have never been inside O'Leary's Funeral Home before.

It smells exactly like Mr. Locker's Greenhouse. Like roses, tons and tons of roses.

Sometimes, when Mother takes naps, you ride your bike down to Locker"s just to smell the flowers. Last time you went, Mr. Locker let you hang out and watch him water the geraniums. He told you he used to work at Titus with your Dad, but after his house burned down, he used the insurance money to build his greenhouse with a small apartment on top. So now, he lives there with his flowers, a white poodle dog named Billie, and lots of fire alarms.

"Queer as a three dollar bill," you once heard your Dad say to Mr. O'Leary when Mr. Locker walked by.

They were out drinking beer on the porch. Mr. Locker waved at them and they waved back, but they busted out laughing as soon as Mr. Locker and Billie turned the corner. It was a mean kind of laugh and it made you sick inside. For some reason you think about last spring when Mr. Novak let you and Hal come with him to Locker's. To pick up two flats of tomatoes. Mr. Novak let Hal ride in the red wagon with the tomatoes. Hal was so happy he didn't want to go home. But when it got dark you made him.

"Where is Hal?" Helen whispers as Aunt Cleo herds you down the carpeted hallway. She plugs her nose. Helen hates roses.

"He is laid out in the far room." Aunt Cleo points to the end of the long carpeted hallway where Mr. O'Leary is standing next to a white door.

"Right down here, folks."

Dad reaches down and brushes Helen's hand away from her nose.

He gives her a look.

There are so many bouquets of roses lined up and down the hallway that their smell makes you dizzy. Helen unplugs her nose, but she gives Dad a look right back.

"This way," Mr. O'Leary says. He is dressed up in a blue suit with a red tie. Behind him people are filing into a large room and he leads all of you into another room adjacent to the large one. On the far side of this room the door is open and you can see into the other room, where people are sitting on peach-colored chairs and speaking in hushed voices. Organ music seeps in from the ceiling.

Dad brings Mother over to a sofa where she can sit.

Mr. O'Leary leans down and says to Dad so softly you can barely hear, "We'll have the family come in last. That way there'll be a little time for visitation."

Mr. O'Leary has a little mustache and huge bushy eye-brows that move up and down when he talks. He glances over at Mother and then looks at you and Helen and Jacob and says, "It shouldn't be too long, kids."

He pats a cushioned bench on his way out the door. The velvet feels soft on your legs as you obediently sit down. Helen sits next to you, but Jacob goes over and tries to sit by Mother, who makes a hissing sound from under her veil.

Dad pushes Jacob away.

"Maybe later, Sport," he says to Jacob.

Dejected, Jacob attempts to sit next to Helen, but she pushes him away too, even more forcefully. Jacob waves his hand in front of Helen's face, doing an imitation of Curly on the Three Stooges. He makes a sound in his throat, "Nuk, nuk, nuk."

This makes you laugh.

"Stop!" Helen cries out.

"ENOUGH!" Dad's voice booms across the small room.

Helen and Jacob freeze.

You gulp a breath.

Aunt Cleo has gone into the other room to talk with people, so she is not there to break up any fights. It is up to you to keep the peace, so you swallow the laugh bubbling up in your throat and you tell Jacob, "Come, sit by me." But Jacob has discovered a box under the bench filled with cowboys and Indians, and settling himself on the printed carpet at your feet, he begins to stage a battle on the floor.

A sound like a small bird weeping comes out from under Mother's veil. Everyone looks, then Dad pats her leg with his big hand and the noise stops.

Music floats in through the open door.

Mr. O'Leary pops his head in. "The reserved seats are in front. Five more minutes and we'll bring the family in." He looks at Mother and then at Dad, then he walks over to Mother. "How about a little water?" he suggests gently.

Mother sniffles under her veil.

"Thank you," Dad's voice quivers, as if he's trying not to cry, too.

Mr. O'Leary goes over to a crystal decanter sitting on the windowsill. Beads of light filter through the water glasses lined up next to it. The light makes a rainbow across Jacob's battlefield and for a split second you think you see a leprechaun standing near his feet. Then you blink your eyes and he disappears.

Did Jacob see him? You'll ask him when Helen is not around, because Jacob won't tell if Helen can hear and make fun of him.

Mr. O'Leary pours a glass of water and hands it to Mother. She takes two yellow pills out of her little black purse, pushes up the veil, places the pills carefully on her tongue and swallows them with the water, then pulls the veil back down.

Her eyes looked puffier than you've ever seen them. No wonder she's wearing a veil. You can't help but feel relieved that no one is making you or Helen wear a veil. Since Vatican II, the girls at Sacred Heart don't have to wear them anymore. Helen sometimes still wears the one she got for her first communion, but you hate anything poking into your head, especially bobby pins.

After five minutes, Mother lets Mr. O'Leary help her to her feet and Dad lines all of you up according to birth order, with Jacob first. Mr. O'Leary leads the way and it feels as if you are marching in a Fourth of July parade, only someone forgot the batons. You walk into the large mostly white room and all the people hush their voices. You follow your family across the carpet to the row of peach-colored chairs.

You see your cousins, and Aunt Emma and some people you recognize from church, but there are many more you don't recognize and it is so quiet it makes you want to yell SHUT UP!—You don't think you can stand one more minute of all these people looking at you until you spot Hal laid out in the tiny powder blue coffin at the front of the room. Then you forget they are even there.

Hal is dressed in a plaid suit and his hands are folded across his chest. Tucked under one arm there is a blue Morgan dog that looks newer than the one he had in his crib before Dad broke it apart.

His fingers look funny. They look waxy and fake. They're wrapped around a powder blue plastic rosary. You doubt if this is really Hal, or at least, if these are really Hal's hands.

Even though everyone is watching, you can't take your eyes off him. You sit down on the squishy peach chair alongside everyone else. Another sound comes out from under Mother's veil.

Jacob points and shouts, "There's Hal."

A rumble of voices erupts behind you and Dad pushes Jacob's hand back down. He leans down and whispers something into Jacob's ear that you can't hear.

Your head begins to reel out the Lord's prayer, *Our Father... who art in heaven... thy kingdom come... thy will... thy will... thy will... be done... be done... be done... as it is in heaven...* and you remember the only-air Hal, who was more real than this Hal. You scan the room for leprechauns but don't see any, and then someone behind you breaks down sobbing so loud you turn around to look, but all you see is a sea of legs and black suits, skirts, and sweaters, and millions and millions of eyes.

The sobs grow louder. There is something familiar about them.

Helen turns, too, and then, with a sense of delight creeping into her voice, she whispers into your ear, "It's Patty."

Patty is Helen's favorite babysitter. You spot her a few rows back, wailing into a white handkerchief. You like Patty too. When she comes to babysit, she lets you eat ice cream right out of the carton. If it's Neapolitan, everyone eats the chocolate first, and Jacob makes pig noises when it's gone, which don't annoy Helen half as much as the Three Stooges.

Thinking about Neapolitan ice cream reminds you of the Novak's candy dish, and you look but you can't see them in the sea of legs.

CHAPTER 9

The Bruises

INSTEAD OF sitting down and being quiet like he should, Jacob jumps up and makes a dash for the casket. "It's Hal, it's Hal!" he shouts.

Dad quickly grabs him back.

Murmurs break out behind you.

Patty sobs louder.

Dad motions Helen to slide over and he plops Jacob back down on the chair between you and Helen. "Sit," he says firmly. For once Jacob listens.

Helen crosses her arms. She doesn't want to move.

From the front row you and Helen and Jacob stare at the little person in the coffin, who doesn't look anything like Hal. His hair looks funny. It looks like straw, and his face looks like clay and his eyes are closed so you can't tell if they are still green. His body looks like it is filled up with wax, like President Lincoln at the wax museum in The Dells.

President Lincoln is the only real dead person you have ever seen. Helen says it wasn't really him, that Dad was just teasing, and that the real President Lincoln's family probably would not donate his body for a tourist attraction in The Dells, especially since he was from Illinois.

From here it almost looks as if the fake Hal is breathing. You close your eyes and imagine him leaping out of the casket and running toward you, laughing, but when you open your eyes again, he hasn't budged.

Mr. O'Leary lights candles beside the casket as Father O'Rourke enters the room carrying a Bible. Father O'Rourke is wearing a long black robe that goes all the way to his feet.

Everybody who isn't already standing stands up.

"Friends, we are gathered here today…."

While Father O'Rourke talks about the Lamb of God and eternal life, you turn around again to look for the Novaks. Dad glances down at you and shakes his head. His face looks so sad and disappointed you immediately turn back around and try not to fidget. You are mad at Dad for throwing away Hal's stuff, but you know how much he needs you.

"Time is the greatest healing balm that our Heavenly Father gives us, and why one so young is called so early is not for us to know…."

You close your eyes as Father O'Rourke's words wash over you. An oddly familiar odor wafts past your nose, its sourness, like ammonia, mixing with the scent of roses and Dad's Old Spice. Jacob wiggles beside you, and tugs at your hand.

"I hafta go."

Your eyes spring open and you sigh. It's already too late. You look up at Dad and Mother. Should you take him to the bathroom, or wait for Father O'Rourke to finish?

Helen looks at Jacob in disgust and plugs her nose.

"I hafta go…." Jacob's lips begin to tremble. Terror lights up his eyes as he glances from you over to Mother. Mother, like everyone else, is busy bowing her head while Father O'Rourke goes on and on about God's eternal kingdom. Jacob doesn't realize that Mother will not spank him in front of all these people and he starts to cry. You put your arm around his shoulder and kiss his ear. "I'll take you," you whisper, grabbing his hand and leading him down the aisle, looking straight ahead so the millions of eyes won't stop you in your track.

Aunt Cleo must have figured out what happened because she follows.

"Jacob had an acci…" the last letters of the word catch in your throat.

Aunt Cleo nods. She puts her good hand on Jacob's shoulder and leads him to the ladies room. Jacob doesn't want to go in, but she makes him. It is the biggest bathroom you've ever seen. It has its own sofa and two plush pink chairs. It's bigger than your living room at home.

"Take those wet things off," you say to Jacob. It will be hard for Aunt Cleo to help him with only one hand. Jacob just stands there, sniffling.

"Am I gonna get spanked?" He keeps trying not to cry but his voice is shaky.

Aunt Cleo strokes his head, "Oh honey, don't cry, why are you crying? No one is going to spank you. It was just an accident. Accidents happen."

Jacob gulps in air. "Accidents happen," he repeats.

Aunt Cleo keeps stroking his head.

When you finally coax the wet things off of him, Aunt Cleo helps you wash them in the sink. She squeezes more water out of Jacob's underwear with one hand than you can do with two.

Aunt Cleo lets you hold the wet things under the hand dryer. The air feels hot on your fingers. She gives Jacob a little hand towel to cover himself and Jacob crawls up onto the plush pink chair to wait. Because Jacob feels shy about being naked, you know Aunt Cleo is trying to give him some privacy, but when he crawls up onto the chair, she sees the bruises on his back and she suddenly looks alarmed.

"Where in the world did you get those bruises, Jacob O'Malley?"

She walks around the chair and looks at his backside.

Jacob shrugs his knobby shoulders. He begins to mimic the blow dryer. "Errrrrrrrrrrrr. Errrrrrrrrrr. Errrrrrrrrrr." He tries to look around and see for himself.

Over the sound of the hair dryer, you say, "We all play rough." That is what Mother told the school nurse when she asked about your eye last year.

The underwear is drying quickly and you hold it up to show Jacob. "See!"

Jacob smiles.

The blower shuts off and you let Jacob push the silver button again to do his pants. Aunt Cleo's eyebrows are all scrunched together. She helps him back into his underwear the best she can while you finish drying the pants.

Aunt Cleo keeps staring at Jacob's bruises. She doesn't say anything. But you can hear her saying something in her head. She thinks something isn't right.

When the pants are dry you hand them to Jacob. "No one will be able to tell."

"Don't tell Mama," Jacob begs.

"I won't."

With her good arm, Aunt Cleo spins Jacob around to face her. "There will be no spankings while I am around," she says looking deeply into his eyes.

Jacob smiles. He lets Aunt Cleo pull him in close for a hug. Her stump arm peeks out of her shirtsleeve.

By the time you get back, there is a long line of people waiting to walk up to the casket and look at Hal.

"After everyone is done we'll say good-bye to Hal," Aunt Cleo says and leads you back to the front row where your empty chairs are waiting. People part to let you through.

Aunt Emma is in line and she whispers to Aunt Cleo, "Everything okay?"

Aunt Cleo nods. She says nothing about Jacob peeing his pants.

Jacob holds your hand. He is still making blow dryer noises, but very quietly, under his breath. So you don't shush him.

Patty is sitting next to Helen, and to your amazement, she is still crying. With one hand she blows her nose into an embroidered handkerchief and with the other she holds Helen's hand.

You look around and it seems that everyone is crying, except your family. Dad sits with his arm around Mother and you can't really tell if Mother is crying or not because of the veil. It almost seems like she might have fallen asleep again.

Who are all these people? What gives them the right to cry? Did they even know Hal? Only you and your family should be crying. But you can't, it's like all the tears inside have evaporated, like when Sister Francis did the science project at school and the water disappeared overnight; it went into the air.

You sit back down and Helen turns to Jacob. "We go up last," she says, and her voice actually sounds nice.

Jacob looks at her.

She points at Hal.

"D-E-A-D," she spells, quietly, to herself.

CHAPTER 10

The Prayer

AFTER FATHER O'Rourke has given everyone directions to Sacred Heart, Mr. O'Leary says it is your family's turn to go up and say good-bye. You line up behind Dad, who is wearing his blue pinstripe church suit. It looks baggy on him and the pant legs sag over his shoes and his tie is blood red, twisted in a knot tight around his neck. Mr. O'Leary waits at the end of the aisle and signals you, one at a time.

The kids go first. Dad steps back holding onto Mother. He nods his approval when you take Jacob's hand. Helen can take care of herself. It will only make her mad if you try to help.

As you walk past Mother, Jacob looks up under her veil and you do, too. She doesn't seem to notice either of you. Despite the puffiness, her eyes are not crazy, yet there is something even scarier about them. They remind you of gun barrels.

Dad seems to be holding Mother up. She presses her fingers into his arm and whispers hoarsely, "I can't."

Dad nods for you to take Jacob and go ahead. He and Mr. O'Leary help Mother back into her chair. Everyone is watching Mother, so you lead Helen and Jacob up to the casket. When you get there, Jacob can barely see over the top and Mr. O'Leary rushes up with a wooden step stool. Jacob steps onto it, still clinging onto your hand.

"Thanks," you tell Mr. O'Leary.

A murmur of voices and some shuffling breaks out behind you and Mr. O'Leary nods and rushes back to Mother, while your eyes zoom in on Hal.

Up close, Hal looks less like a wax mannequin and more like a plastic doll. His face is caked with powder and his hair is combed down over his forehead, like Frankenstein. Helen glances over at you. She is thinking the same thing. "Is he really dead?"

You shrug.

"This is a fake Hal!"

You agree, but don't say so.

Jacob starts humming, "Errrrrrrrmmm. Errrrrrmm…."

Helen puts her fingers to her ears.

"Shush," you lean over near Jacob and put your finger to your lips. On the step stool, Jacob stands eye to eye with you and he blinks.

"Hal got hit by a car… he's dead… it was an accident… accidents happen," he sings softly, but he's looking past you.

"Duh," Helen's fingers are out of her ears and she narrows her eyes at him.

To fend off a fight you squeeze Jacob's hand. "Yes, it was an accid—"

Jacob's squeezes your hand in desperation, "Right!"

"Right."

Suddenly there is a loud commotion behind you. All three of you turn around to see Dad and Mr. O'Leary helping Mother up off the floor. Mother tries to shake them off and crumples into a ball, but they each grab one of her arms and rush her back to the small room where Jacob's cowboys and Indians are still set up on the floor.

The sea of black behind you begins to undulate, low utterances and gasps break out behind you. Aunt Cleo and Father O'Rourke, who were helping with Mother, join you three kids at the casket as people begin to filter out the back door so your family has privacy for the final good-bye.

"They are going to close the casket soon," Father O'Rourke says quietly, "but you kids take as long as you need." He leaves you alone with Aunt Cleo. She places her good hand on your shoulder and her stump on Helen's while Jacob snuggles in the middle. The sound behind you fades away. All you can hear is the sound of Aunt Cleo's lips above your head brushing together in a halo of prayer.

Aunt Cleo believes in the power of prayer. She claims prayers are more powerful than the atom bomb and that every one gets answered.

You wish you believed in them the way Aunt Cleo does. If you could pray hard enough, maybe Hal would come back to life. So you close your eyes and concentrate with all your might and make a prayer, which is really more like a wish, that when you open your eyes, Hal will be alive. Not the only-air Hal. Not the waxy fake Hal. The real Hal.

Someone coughs.

When you turn around everyone has left and Father O'Rourke is sitting in a fancy chair at the back of the room. He looks at you with watery eyes.

You look back at Hal: he is not alive. Then your eyes meet Father O'Rourke's. You want to ask him why God took Hal, why God needs more angels in heaven when he's got so many. But Father O'Rourke looks so sad and tired you decide just to pray again.

"Errrrrrrrrrrr—"

Jacob starts his noises. Helen reaches over and slaps her hand over his mouth. He stops. He doesn't even know he's doing it. She lets her hand drop and closes her eyes like Aunt Cleo. Jacob does, too. You join them, wondering if they are praying for the same thing.

The Lord's Prayer begins to circle around in your head and its words get mixed up with yours: *Our Father if you let Hal live I will never never never leave him alone... never never never... our Father... who art in heaven.... I will never swear or lie or do any of the sins of the Ten Commandments... never never never.... if you can hear me God and Jesus and the Holy Ghost... please please please... let Hal live again.... If you need more kids in heaven... I will come.... I am the oldest... and God, please tell Jesus... I am sorry for leaving Hal... even though Dad told me to.... and please please please forgive Dad for not taking us to church, even though it was a sin.... and help Mother not to go crazy.... and tell Mr. Novak it wasn't his fault... and I am sorry I didn't eat Mrs. Novak's potato pancakes.... and I will go to confession every week and please please please Jesus.... I promise to take good care of Helen and Jacob.... I am the oldest.... I promise to be better.... I am sorry for leaving Hal.... if you*

*make everything okay... I will never never never leave Hal
again... never... never... never... not even if Dad says—*
   "The procession can begin whenever you're ready." Mr.
O'Leary comes up and stands beside Aunt Cleo.
   What's a *procession?* Then Aunt Cleo nods. You look at
Hal—he is still not breathing! He still looks fake, made
of plastic, and you can feel a coldness creeping in around
your heart.
   Aunt Cleo must be wrong when she says God answers all
prayers. If it were true, why is Hal not breathing?
   "Are you going to lock it?" Jacob points at the casket.
   Mr. O'Leary pats Jacob's back.
   "Are you?" Jacob asks insistently, "Are you going to
lock it?"
   Mr. O'Leary looks like he is trying to understand. "Do
you want to help me close it?"
   Jacob nods. "And lock it."
   Aunt Cleo finishes her prayer and then pulls you and
Helen away from the casket so Jacob can help Mr. O'Leary.
Helen loosens herself from Aunt Cleo and wanders back
into the room where Mother and Dad are waiting. Helen is
not crying, but her eyes look funny, in a different way than
Mothers. Like fly eyes that never blink.
   Helen sits down on the bench. Her eyes keep staring
and staring and staring, but she is not looking at anything.
You know she is remembering Hal. How he was when
he was alive. How he never learned not to cry. How mad
that made Mother, and how Helen hated the sound of it.
Is that why she plugs her ears all the time? Perhaps. All you
know for sure is that neither you, nor Helen, can stand the

sound of anyone crying. You go back into the big room to get Jacob.

"Where's the lock?" Jacob looks up at Mr. O'Leary as they close the casket. "If you don't lock it, Hal will hafta shrink down into Mama's tummy again."

Mr. O'Leary gazes down at Jacob. You wonder how dark it is inside that casket. What will happen if the prayer really works and Hal starts breathing again and he wakes up and he can't get out?

In New Jersey where Aunt Cleo used to live with Grandmother Golding, there is a cemetery where a long time ago people got some kind of sleeping sickness and everyone thought they were dead, so they buried them, but then, the people weren't really dead and they woke up inside their caskets and when the workers came to relocate the graves for the turnpike to come through, they discovered that some of the people woke up and tried to claw their way out.

You are not sure you like Jacob's lock idea. But Jacob keeps hanging onto the casket and staring at Mr. O'Leary. "Hal doesn't want to hafta…."

Gently, Mr. O'Leary puts his hand on Jacob's shoulder.

"I have a lock… I'll put it on later, I promise."

Mr. O'Leary is lying. But this seems to satisfy Jacob and he lets go and Mr. O'Leary rolls the casket to a back door, where a long black car is idling. Aunt Cleo shuffles you back into the small room where Helen sits staring and Dad and Mother are waiting.

Mother sniffles under her veil and Dad sits next to her smoking a cigarette. Over and over again he rubs his hands together as if warming them up to pray, but Dad doesn't pray. Doesn't even believe in prayers. Once he said he goes to church to keep Mother happy. And, if there is a God, that God helps those who help themselves. Mother hates when he says stuff like this. She hates that he doesn't want to go to church. They get in huge fights about it—like on the morning of the accident.

When Mother gets mad she goes crazy. She especially hates the Green Bay Packers because they always play on Sundays when Dad is supposed to be helping out.

Dad believes watching the Packers is like going to church and that Vince Lombardi will go down in history as one of the greatest coaches of all time. That this is history in the making.

"Where are they taking Hal?" you ask Dad.

"To church," Aunt Cleo replies.

The back door is still open and the sky is very blue behind the black car and Hal's white casket is resting on two silver bars in the back.

Aunt Cleo sits down on the bench, meaning all of you should do the same. Dad doesn't say anything. He takes long slow puffs on his cigarette, staring straight ahead. You go and sit on the bench next to Helen, but Jacob kneels on the floor and starts to play with the cowboys and Indians.

Your mind keeps leapfrogging between football and church. You think about Bart Starr, the quarterback of the Green Bay Packers. Dad brought you and Helen and Jacob to get his autograph at the JC Penney's store. There was a long line and when you got up to the table Helen refused to take the picture because she thinks football is stupid. Dad took one for her and she ripped it up in the back seat on the way back home.

Dad didn't spank her.

Dad never spanks hard, but sometimes at night he'll say, "Now be good or your Mother will come in here," and that does make Helen afraid. When Mother comes into your room at night it is never good. And if Mother is really mad it is a lot worse to be there in the dark. You don't even like to think about the dark, but sometimes you do even when you try not to.

Dark. Dark. Dark.

You stare through the door at Hal's casket. It is still resting in the back of the car. The inside must be very dark because there are no windows or openings and if Hal does wake up it will be pitch dark and if—

"May! Come along."

Somehow, everyone else is headed out of the room and down the hall. You leap to your feet and race to catch up with Aunt Cleo.

The tall limo man swings open the door for Mother and Dad.

"Easy now," he says to them.

Helen runs up to him and tries to take his hand.

"Just a second there, missy," he says. First, he opens the car door for Mother, then his big stork legs climb back up the steps and he takes Helen's hand and leads her down the steps. Jacob just jumps inside the compartment. You and Aunt Cleo follow. After you're settled in, you reach across Aunt Cleo and lock the door from the inside.

Her stump arm is facing the window and she can't lock the door on her own.

CHAPTER 11

The Church

THIS TIME, even though it is Friday, the limo takes you to Sacred Heart. You never go to church on Friday, except on Good Friday, when Fr. O'Rourke tells the story of Jesus getting hung on the cross and how God made the sky turn dark in the middle of the day.

Dark. Dark. Dark.

Try not to think about it.

Outside the limo window it is not dark. It is a blue-blue sky with no clouds and the trees that arch over the road have started to turn orange and red and gold. Pretty soon Aunt Emma will organize a leaf-raking party with home-made apple cider, but all you think about is...

Dark. Dark. Dark.

You try to focus on the line of cars in front of the limo with their tiny yellow funeral flags flapping in the wind, but your brain flips around like a fish, making you think about the darkness inside of Hal's casket.

Dark. Dark. Dark.

You squeeze your eyes tightly and when you open them you see Mother absentmindedly push her veil up over her head, so she can breathe better. No one tries to talk to her. She keeps her eyes closed. Jacob's stuffed his pockets with cowboys and Indians, and now, instead of bugging Mother, he empties them onto the limo floor where he lines them up and hums a marching song. It sounds suspiciously like the marching song he sings for the ants, the one that Helen hates.

It doesn't matter, though, because Helen has her head tucked in the crook of Aunt Cleo's stump and she's got her ears plugged, ignoring Jacob.

When you finally arrive at Sacred Heart, the lights inside the church are turned down low. There are even more roses along the aisle than there were at O'Leary's, in fact, so many roses that Helen sneezes.

"Ah chooo!"

Aunt Cleo fishes a lace hanky from her purse and holds it out for Helen to take. Helen refuses because she sees some of Aunt Cleo's tears are already on it and she doesn't want to touch it.

"Honey, the polite thing to do is cover your mouth." Aunt Cleo jiggles the hanky in front of Helen's face.

Helen crinkles her eyes and stares, shaking her head slowly from side to side.

"Ah chooo!" A huge rope of snot flies out of Helen's nose onto the front of her dress.

"See?" To Helen's horror, Aunt Cleo deftly uses her one strong hand to wipe Helen's nose.

"No—" Helen starts crying, but the soggy hanky has already obliterated her face as everyone begins to clomp down the stone floor toward the front of the church. Helen tags along, tears streaming down her cheeks.

You want to make her feel better, so you point to the sign on the end of the front pew. "What's it say?"

"Reserved," she coughs out hoarsely.

Sometimes Helen amazes you. She is so smart. It seems to you that she can read almost any word, even big ones. You let her genuflect and go into the pew first; still sniffling, she slides past, not letting her eyes meet yours.

Your cousins and Aunt Emma and the relatives you know from bingo parties at Uncle Bob's bar are already scattered in the pews along with a million people you do not know. No one waves or makes a big fuss. Mr. O'Leary and another man from the funeral home roll Hal's casket down the center aisle to the front of the church. The wheels of the cart under Hal's coffin sound exactly like the wheels of the red wagon.

You hear a man from Dad's work say, "Ah, what a damn bloody shame. It's hardly bigger than a bread box."

Before you remember who that man is, you spot the Novaks about ten rows back, sitting next to the McLaughlins, who have the most children of any family in Pig Valley. Twelve of them, but you only know the three who go to Sacred Heart. Their dad works at Titus Tannery, too. Sometimes he comes over and drinks beer on the front porch with your dad, and they talk about when JFK got shot, and the Vietnam War, and how two of Mr. McLaughlin's boys got drafted.

The Novaks are dressed almost entirely in black. Except Mr. Novak is wearing a thin white dress shirt with the gold cuff links. His shirt sleeves are pulled down over the little blue numbers that don't wash off. Mrs. Novak has on white gloves so you can't see her marks either. They look so small and out of place it makes you wonder if they have ever been inside a Catholic church.

You lean over to Helen. "Do Jewish people have churches?"

Helen's face is red and streaky. She nods, but she still doesn't look at you. She whispers back, "They're called Sin-a-Gods." This seems like a strange name, but you'll get in trouble if you try to talk more in church.

Everyone is supposed to be quiet, that's why there is a crying room for the babies. Now Hal can't cry anymore, so he will never have to go to the crying room again.

CHAPTER 12

The Time Pockets

YOU LOOK up at the front altar where the huge wood-carved Jesus rests on the cross. He is almost as tall as a house. The only thing covering his private parts is a little piece of carved cloth. You wonder if the Novaks know that Jesus was a Jew, or about the people in the Bible who wanted Pontius Pilot to kill Jesus because of it. Do they even know that Jesus rose from the dead to save everyone's sins?

When Mass starts, Fr. O'Rourke comes in wearing the same shiny black robe, only he's added a sparkly gold scarf and a hat shaped like an upside down bowling ball bag. The Mass is half over when he goes behind the altar and brings out a smoking silver ball on a long silver chain. The smoke curls up around his head and soon the entire church smells like burning pine needles, and Fr. O'Rourke waves the ball around Hal's coffin and chants. Then he waves the ball at the altar and chants some more, and finally he walks up and down all the aisles waving it in the direction of all the people. There are so many people in the church it takes him a long time to wave the smoking ball at everyone.

You wait, squeezing your eyes, trying not to think about dark things, like the inside of Hal's casket. People all around you shuffle and cough and clear their throats. It takes a lot of concentration not to think about things you do not want to be thinking about, but your head keeps hopping around with all kinds of thoughts. What will happen if God decides to answer your prayer, if he does bring Hal back to life?

Like Jesus.

If God does bring Hal back, Hal will definitely smell the silver ball, because the church is even smokier than the time Dad soaked the bratwurst in beer and left them out on the grill too long and they started on fire and the wind blew the black smoke into the house and made the bed sheets smell like burned meat, including Jacob's. But that was an improvement over how they usually smelled.

You didn't mind the smoky smell but it made Mother mad, so you helped Dad pick the burned skin off and cut them up for dinner. They still tasted juicy and next to chocolate milk, bratwursts are Hal's favorite food, so he sniffed at them and ate them, anyway.

Hal sniffed everything. His food. His shirts. His Morgan dog. Especially his blue blanket.

You feel glad Hal's blue blanket is in the casket with him. You open your eyes again and remember last spring. Mother sent you and Hal over to Mrs. Shannon's house to help pick lily of the valley flowers.

Mrs. Shannon needed help because lily of the valley flowers have tons of roots that grow like weeds and take over everything. Hal brought home a fistful and kept sniffing them and sniffing them until the tip of his nose turned yellow. Mother let him take the flowers into his crib for naptime, but after he fell asleep, she made you take them back outside so God would turn them into dirt.

You knew Hal would remember them, so you put them behind the garage in the secret hideout. That way he could find them again if he wanted.

As Father O'Rourke wanders up and down flicking the smoky ball, Helen coughs and Aunt Cleo tries to hand her the hanky again. Helen leans her head into Aunt Cleo's side instead, and Aunt Cleo hugs her and rocks her, and Helen starts to cry.

Helen cries more than anyone else in the family.

Sometimes, when she cries, it makes you feel like you want to cry too, but you don't.

You are the oldest.

When you look over, Mother is sitting stone-still on the edge of the wooden pew with her hands folded in her lap. Dad is standing like everyone else, and his hands rest on the back of the pew in front of you. The scars that have healed over from his work at Titus Tannery look like lots of little white lightning bolts on his skin. For years he worked with a knife and a big cutting machine, but he got promoted to manager, so now he only tells people how to skin the animals.

Jacob is in his own little world. He squats on the kneeler, playing with the cowboys and Indians on the pew. No one makes him stop humming because he is doing it so softly and he has switched to a new song that sounds more like the ocean in a seashell.

When Father O'Rourke is done waving the ball, it is time for communion, which means Mass is almost over and everyone, except Mother, gets ready to go up to the front of the church to receive communion. You had your first communion last year, so you follow Dad and Aunt Cleo as they shuffle down to the end of the pew. Mother doesn't budge so everyone lets her be.

When Father O'Rourke puts the wafer on your tongue and says, "Body of Christ," you are supposed to say, "Amen," but you don't, because part of you is mad at God. It is a sin not to believe in God, but just in case you cross yourself like everyone.

Then, you decide that maybe you don't want to be friends with a God who lets babies die, and then for some reason you decide to see how long the wafer will last in your mouth. So you try to swallow all the spit down into the back of your throat, because the spit makes it melt, and you walk back to the pew trying not to look conspicuous. This is one of the words you learned in Hangman, though you don't know how to spell it.

The Novaks look straight ahead as you walk by. They did not go up for communion. Probably, they are wondering how long the Mass will last.

Once, your best friend Yvonne kept a wafer on the roof of her mouth all morning, and then at lunch took it out and put it in her peanut butter sandwich. Sean O'Connel, the smartest kid at Sacred Heart, told on her, because it was a sin. That afternoon, Sister Francis made Yvonne's parents come to Sacred Heart and they had to have a special meeting and take Yvonne to confession so she wouldn't end up condemned to eternal damnation.

Yvonne got so mad at Sean that she put a brick in her purse and brought it to school the next day. At recess, she tried to swing it at his head like a lasso, but Sean hid out in the tunnel and hollered Bible verses.

Later Sean said Yvonne should thank him for saving her immortal soul and making sure she would not rot in hell. But Yvonne said Sacred Heart Elementary School was her definition of a personal hell, so she was already there.

In the month that followed, Sister Francis gave dozens of quizzes on hell and the difference between mortal and venial sins. She said the words *immortal soul* 768 times.

That had to be some kind of record.

The sound of Sister Francis' voice saying *immortal soul* starts to flip around in your brain along with other images of dark things—the dark cellar in the basement, the dark color of Mother's favorite beer, the dark skin of the limo driver, the dark spot on the kitchen floor. Then, somehow, though you don't know how it happens, church is over and you are back in the limo headed to the graveyard and you don't even remember walking to the car, and the wafer has melted!

You postulate, which is a lot like pondering, only more scientific and more acceptable according to Sister Francis, that the wafer has magical powers because of transubstantiation, which means the priest makes it turn into the real body and blood of Jesus. Even though it still looks like a wafer. Transubstantiation is the biggest word ever spelled in the history of Hangman at Sacred Heart. You'll probably never be able to spell it for another million years, but you remember what it means. And perhaps the wafer somehow knew what you were planning to do and it didn't want you to get in trouble, so it melted itself away and put you into a time pocket.

Time pockets never happen to Helen. But they happen to you all the time.

Mostly, at night. Sometimes they happen when the Star People come.

Helen can't always see the Star People. Though she believes you when you tell her when they are standing right next to your bed.

Once you asked the Star People why time pockets only happen to you and they told you in their language that most people have time pockets but they don't remember them, especially grown-ups. So you never talk to any grown-ups about them because they might put you back in the Special Ed class. You have to go there sometimes, because Sister Francis says that although you are perfectly intelligent, your refusal to read must be some odd bid for attention, because when she asks you, you almost always know the answers. Being in the Special Ed class is supposed to remind you of the consequences of willfulness.

You never mention time pockets to Sister Francis.

Helen says they probably happen to you because even though you are sort of smart, you can't read, which makes teachers think you're dumb. But you know a lot of things, like when Mother's in a bad mood and when it's better to stay outside and play, and if it's Aunt Cleo on the phone, and even if the Packers will win. Dad won a hundred dollars when you guessed right.

As the limo drives over the bridge, you see Yvonne out riding her new pink banana seat bike. You want to wave, but the windows are tinted and she can't see inside.

Does Yvonne know about Hal?

Did she tell all the other kids at Sacred Heart?

Yvonne is the first person who ever kissed you on the lips. She did it at the slumber party on her birthday. You were so surprised you swallowed the Tootsie Roll in your mouth without even chewing it.

Yvonne lives in a bungalow house by the river behind Pig Valley. She has her own bedroom because she has no brothers or sisters, and because her real dad got shot in Vietnam. She can't really remember her real dad, which makes you feel a little sorry for her. But now she has a new dad, the one who bought her the bike, and even though she says he bought it as a bribe so she would like him, Yvonne hates him anyway.

You met him once. He's a police officer. He seemed sort of nice. So you told Yvonne it was a sin for her to hate her parents, but she said her new dad didn't count, and besides, she had decided to be an atheist, and not to believe in God, period.

Next to Sean, Yvonne is the second smartest kid in sixth grade. She says nobody should worry about sins, even if they do believe in God, because all Catholics can go to confession and get them wiped away. Yvonne says even mass murderers like the guy who ate the people he killed, and made their skin into lampshades, could go.

Yvonne said even if she did believe in God, it would be okay to hate someone, as long as she confessed it.

This does make some sense to you.

Then, it occurs to you. You could go to confession and ask God to forgive you for leaving Hal. For not telling Mr. Novak, even though the coconut clogged up your throat and Babushka made everyone laugh, that you knew it wasn't his fault. Even if his stupid car did hit Hal, you shouldn't have left him.

Hal was only two years old.

That's barely anything.

God should have taken you, you are the oldest and you are not afraid of the dark.

CHAPTER 13

The Black Boy

THE LIMO drives further and further into the city. Pretty soon the houses begin to look worn out and ragged. When the limo stops at a light, you see three black men laughing and throwing something against the stoop outside of a bar. One is wearing a plastic bag on his head. You want to ask Helen the name of the bar. There's a letter you recognize—it's one of your favorites—because when you turn it upside down it makes an M, which is the first letter in your name. But Helen has fallen asleep under Aunt Cleo's stump arm and you don't want to wake her.

You scoot closer to the window. The men are smiling and laughing and throwing pennies. How stupid. Why would poor people throw pennies on the sidewalk?

In Pig Valley no one would ever throw pennies, even if they were poor.

Once your Dad took you to visit Lilly, who came to help when Mother was in the hospital. Dad made you stay in the car with the locks down because he said it was too dangerous. You waited forever, and when Dad didn't come out you got out of the car and stood on the sidewalk.

A boy came out onto his porch and said, "Hey, what you doin'?"

You yelled back, "My dad is talking to Lilly."

He was wearing a sleeveless T-shirt that was way too big. It had a number 33 and the name *Jerome* written on it with black marker.

"How you know Lilly?" he demanded.

"She comes to help," you said.

You wanted to ask if he knew that the number 33 belonged to Kareem Abdul Jabbar, who lives in a house with 9-foot doors just two blocks from Pig Valley, but his eyes made you feel jumpy, and he just stared and stared and stared. It felt like he was going to stand there forever and just stare and stare and stare.

"I'm May," you finally said, hoping Dad wouldn't come out and catch you. "I go to Sacred Heart," you added as an afterthought. You sensed that he was a little afraid too, and when he didn't say anything back, you got back in the car and locked the doors like Dad said.

On the way home, skipping the part about getting out of the car, you told Dad about the boy.

"Pumpkin," he said that day, "those folks would just as soon slit your throat as look at you."

Now you look over at your dad. He is holding onto Mother's hand and looking out the window. His eyes are watery and it makes you sad, so you look away.

CHAPTER 14

The Graveyard

AT THE graveyard there are miles and miles of stones with people's names carved on them. Aunt Cleo points out Grandpa JJ's stone. She holds you and Helen and Jacob back to give Dad time to settle Mother in a chair.

People stream in bringing bouquets of flowers from church and putting them all around the hole in the ground. Mr. O'Leary and some of his helpers place Hal's casket on a band of ropes. There's a crank on the end directly above the dark opening in the earth. A sick feeling sloshes around in your stomach. This is where they are going to put Hal?

The hole looks dark.

Later, Aunt Cleo says not everyone from church came to the graveyard. But people keep coming and coming and coming, and they are whispering and sniffling and making a giant circle around the grave. Somewhere behind you, Patty starts to sob again.

"We ask you Heavenly Father…." Father O'Rourke starts to pray. Other people, besides Patty, start to cry too, and for a moment Mother's veil blows up off her face and you see her eyes are closed, but you know she is not sleeping, she is not even praying. She's waiting for this to be over. She wants to go home and go to sleep. She's trying to remember how many of the little blue pills she can take.

She can take three at a time.

Dad is wearing his sunglasses, and you can't see if he is crying, but you can feel his sadness. You put your hand in his and squeeze and he squeezes back. His hand feels hot even though the air outside is getting colder.

The wind begins to blow and some red and gold and yellow leaves race across the top of your patent leather shoes, and a few of them blow down into the freshly dug grave and you spot a worm sticking halfway out of the dirt.

You try not to think about the fact that time is running out. If God is going to make a miracle happen he'd better hurry.

The worm makes you let go of Dad's hand and crouch down to see if it got cut in half by a shovel. The wind picks up and flaps the canvas cover over Hal's coffin. Fr. O'Rourke speaks loudly so people can hear over the flapping and snapping. He takes his silver wand and walks around sprinkling holy water into the hole and over everyone's heads.

An ice-cold raindrop of water hits your cheek.

"From dust we were created, to dust shall we return…."

You stand up and let Fr. O'Rourke through. Aunt Cleo signals you to come, so you go stand beside her, Helen, and Jacob.

The wind carries the scent of winter and the smell of dying trees. The trees will only sleep until spring, but you feel sad for them anyway. You lick the holy water off your lip. It tastes like the soda you had at the Novak's house. You look around but don't see them.

You point at the worm for Helen and Jacob, but they are busy watching Fr. O'Rourke.

Mr. O'Leary hands Dad a shovel and then nods to his assistant. They slowly begin to turn the crank that lowers Hal's casket into the ground. Dad walks over and digs the shovel deep into the pile of dirt. The worm gets picked up. Dad holds the dirt and the worm over the hole. Another gust of wind blows most of the dirt off the shovel into the hole, along with some leaves, but Dad just stands there like a statue. Mr. O'Leary comes and puts his hand on Dad's shoulder. Finally, Dad clears his throat and dumps the dirt onto Hal's coffin.

Clumpity. Clump. Clump.

It's a weird hollow sound.

Gently, Mr. O'Leary takes the shovel and shoves it back into the dirt. All around you people make the sign of the cross. Most of them are holding onto their hats and heading back to their cars. Some back away near the trees to stay and talk quietly. Jacob picks up the shovel, but Mr. O'Leary rushes over and takes it. Mr. O'Leary points to a big front-end loader parked behind the canvas tent. He whispers into Jacob's ear, "The truck will do the rest."

"Is it locked? Did you put the lock on?"

Jacob is too close to the edge of the hole and you get behind him just in case he gets any crazy ideas. But he's peering down at the casket to see if Mr. O'Leary really did lock it.

Mr. O'Leary acts like he doesn't hear. He hands the shovel to his assistant.

It's too dark down in the hole to tell if there really is a lock or not, but you can see the worm. This makes you wonder if the worm will get into the casket and bother Hal, and you try to remember if worms hibernate, and this gets you thinking about how cold the wind feels and wondering if Hal's bones will freeze and crack like sidewalks in the wintertime.

At least if his bones do crack he won't feel it.

Once in a magazine at Aunt Emma's house Helen showed you pictures of famous people who paid money to have their bodies frozen. That way they could come back to life in the future. Why didn't Mr. O'Leary answer Jacob? What if Jacob is right, what if instead of dying, people kind of hibernate in their graves? Then, God shrinks them, and somehow puts them into their mother's stomach? What if God forgot to shrink them? Maybe that's why the dead people in the cemetery near Aunt Cleo's house woke up and tried to scratch their way out.

You start to feel panicky inside. What if God does decide to bring Hal back to life after he's already buried? Lock or no lock, with all that dirt on top, he wouldn't be able get out.

You say a prayer in your head. *God, please, you have to hurry!*

"May, Jacob, come along." Aunt Cleo herds you and Jacob back to the limo. Helen is already standing next to the car, holding the limo driver's hand, and you don't look at them because you don't want to stare at his pink palms.

"His name is Al," Helen says, "and he likes ice cream."

You nod.

"Chocolate or vanilla?" Jacob asks him.

He smiles, "Chocolate, son, always chocolate."

"Me too," Jacob agrees.

Aunt Cleo smiles. Then everybody just stands there quietly waiting for Mother and Dad.

You close your eyes and lean up against the door of the car. What if when you get back home everything is like it was before Hal died? What if you're just in a time pocket? Then you will take Hal to Aunt Emma's house, no matter what Dad says.

You imagine putting Hal in the red wagon and looking both ways and wheeling him across Point Road. You can hear the sounds of the cars on Point Road and the squeak of the wagon wheels and Jacob humming a marching song. You take Hal to play with your cousins in the woods behind Aunt Emma's house and you help feed him graham crackers with butter as a snack on Aunt Emma's back porch. Later you go to the river and take his shoes and socks off and dip his toes into the cold water. You imagine him laughing, and you look into his green eyes and hold him up and tell him that you love him.

You will never ever ever let anything bad happen to him.

Never. Ever.

Then you can't help thinking about all the "ifs." *If* Dad didn't want to watch a stupid Packer game, *if* your family had gone to church, *if* Mother hadn't gone crazy, *if* you'd taken Hal to Aunt Emma's house, *if* the Novaks hadn't gone to the store, *if* Hal had stayed asleep on the braid rug, *if* he hadn't tried to run away. So many "ifs" make you dizzy.

Suddenly, Dad's voice is telling everyone it is time to go and Aunt Cleo is trying to get you into the limo and the whole family is going to just leave. You look back at the grave and God has done nothing!

Not a single miracle!

After your family drives off, the front-end loader will put all the dirt on top of Hal and there is no lock on the stupid casket and the worms will get in and bother Hal and Aunt Cleo is a liar because God doesn't answer every prayer and all Helen cares about is holding the limo driver's hand and all Jacob wants is to play with his stupid cowboys and Indians, and all Mother thinks about is her blue pills. And Dad says, "Come on May, get in," because he has settled Mother in. But you just stand there. Staring at the grave.

"May?"

You don't move.

You don't even look at him.

He's trying to make you leave Hal again and you won't.

"For God's sake, make her get in the car." Mother's voice comes from the little compartment in the back.

"May, listen to your Mother," Dad says, his voice shaky and a little scared, but you know Mother won't go crazy in front of the limo driver or Aunt Cleo so you turn around and run as fast as you can straight back to the grave.

"HAL!" You holler in case he has woken up. Can he hear you? You run up to the edge of the hole and yell down, "HAL, it's me!"

Mr. O'Leary grabs you by the arm. His hands are almost as strong as Dad's.

"May, it's better if you go now."

He starts to pull you back and Dad hurries toward you.

"THERE'S NO LOCK!" You are yelling to Hal or God or even Jacob, because Hal is going to freeze and crack and rot down there if no one does anything.

Dad grabs your other arm and you start to flail and kick at them.

"NO! I won't leave him! I won't!"

Dad crouches down and shakes you. "Calm down!"

"It's your fault Hal's dead, you made me leave him. He's dead because of the stupid Packers and now God is mad because we didn't go to church and now there won't be any miracles. It's all your fa—"

Dad's huge hand broadsides your face. Your head snaps back and heat explodes across your face.

"Jesus, May!" he cries, then pulls you into his chest. "Calm down, please calm down," he starts to cry.

But even though he has never slapped your face before, and even though it was hard, and it hurt terribly, you don't cry. You are the oldest and you are never going to leave Hal again. Never. Then he picks you up and carries you back to the limo. He is too strong to push away, so you let your body go limp.

Over his shoulder you see Hal's grave and the little canvas tent flapping in the wind. They are bouncing away from you. You close your eyes and try to listen, to see if Hal did wake up, but all you hear is the wind and Dad's breathing and the low rumble of the idling limo.

At the limo, Dad sets you down carefully, his giant hands resting on your shoulders.

Everyone is waiting.

Dad says, "Hal is up in heaven and there isn't more we can do."

Your eyes meet his. This must be what it is like to hate someone.

"We can't leave him," you whisper.

"May. He's already gone."

You know it is true. You hate him because it is the one true thing he has said since the accident, and all the protein Aunt Cleo fed you for breakfast starts to rumble and you throw up all over your patent leather shoes and all over the grass.

"Ahh." Jacob is leaning out the limo window.

Aunt Cleo pulls him back in and leans out to hand Dad her hanky.

Dad wipes at your mouth with the hanky and you can taste sour spit and Velveeta cheese. He guides you into the limo, then steps in himself, and shuts the door. You close your eyes so you won't cry.

When the limo driver drops you back at home, you dash for the bathroom, afraid you might throw up again. You don't, but you keep burping up Velveeta cheese. After a while, Dad comes into the bathroom. He holds you out in front of him. "Now I'm going to need my best helper, you understand?"

You nod.

"Aunt Cleo has to go home. Can I count on you to get Helen and Jacob to bed while I take care of your Mother?"

You nod again.

"From now on, we'll all have to pitch in and take care of Mother, so she doesn't—

"Have to go back to the hospital and be in a wheelchair," you finish.

He nods. "That's my girl." He hands you your frog pajamas.

"Why is there a blood spot on the kitchen floor?" you ask.

He looks surprised. His face screws up. "What blood spot?"

"The one by Jacob and Hal's door."

"There's no bl—

"I'll show—

He puts his hand up. "Stop, May. Be a good girl. Put your pajamas on. Go to bed."

After he leaves, you stand on the toilet seat to look at your teeth in the mirror. They don't look dirty, but you can still taste the Velveeta cheese so you swipe toothpaste directly onto your mouth and screw the cap back on and swish it around with water. The toothpaste tastes a little like Bazooka Joe bubble gum. If Dad checks your tooth-brush he'll see it is not wet. But you doubt he will.

Long after Helen has fallen asleep, you lie awake in the top bunk. You are thinking about the blood spot. You wonder how it got there and who puts all these questions in your brain.

Most of all you wonder what kind of lie your father is telling.

CHAPTER 15

The Blind Man

IT TAKES almost an entire year before you mention the blood spot to Helen. Ever since the day of the accident it's like part of her brain went into a closet and never came out. Now, she doesn't talk to you, or anyone else in the family, anymore. It's like she's a ghost, but she's still alive.

At night, even though she doesn't answer you, you still talk to her, just like you used to before the accident. Sometimes it seems like she is listening, and sometimes, she just curls up in the bottom bunk, puts her pillow over her head, and plugs her ears.

The night you talk about the spot it is pitch black in your room. Dad has put a blanket over the window to keep heat in, and though you're not sure Helen is listening, she says, "I didn't see the spot, but I heard."

"Heard what?" you whisper into the darkness, surprised after all these months to hear her voice. She doesn't answer. Soon her breathing gets soft and you know that she is asleep in the bunk below you, so you drift off too, wondering what Helen heard and why she doesn't talk anymore.

The next day on the way home from school Helen talks again, but this time all she says is she doesn't want to walk home from school with you anymore. She has a new best friend who is in sixth grade who is named Marie. She only wants to walk with Marie.

"Marie is *my* friend and I don't want you interfering," Helen says. As she slings her pink backpack over the shoulder of her pink winter coat, she leaves you standing there next to the row of lockers.

Ever since the day of the accident, it feels like Helen hates you. Like she knows Hal is dead because of you, but she's not saying so, and even if she doesn't want you to be her sister, you always will be. No matter what. It's just the way it is.

Even though you have different colored eyes, you have matching coats, only yours is blue, because when you went to the store with Mother and Aunt Cleo, who came all the way California for a visit, you refused to try the pink one on. You hate pink. Mother got mad. With Aunt Cleo there, she didn't say anything, but after Aunt Cleo left she pinched your arm until it felt like it would break.

She scrunched up her face, "Don't you ever pull a stunt like that again," she said.

What makes her get like that?

Aunt Cleo stayed for a month, and this made Mother nicer for a while.

When you got in trouble about the coat, Helen laughed. Lately, it seems she likes it when you get in trouble. Now that Helen is talking again, she told Mother, "Pink is my favorite color," and when Mother hugged her, Helen stuck her tongue out and mouthed the word *stupid*.

Sometimes you do feel stupid. But you don't like Helen saying so.

Ever since the accident everybody hates you.

Why did you listen to Dad?

You shouldn't have left Hal.

It's all your fault.

You are not sure what Helen means when she says she doesn't want you interfering, so you say, "I like to walk by myself, anyway."

A part of this is true. You are happy not to have to worry about watching her all the time. And Jacob takes piano lessons every day after school because his teacher figured out he can read music without ever learning how. So you don't have to worry about him either. Best of all, Helen doesn't have to wait around and act all smart because she's reading her chapter books while Ms. Leggly tutors you.

"You'd better learn fast, because I'm not going to wait around for you all the time. And you better not flunk, because I don't want you in my class next year, either."

Ms. Leggly says there is no way you'll flunk seventh grade. If you keep on track, by the time high school rolls around, you'll be at the head of the pack.

You think about Hal as you watch Helen walk away, and how you and Helen used to hurry home so you could help

Mother take care of him after school. Then you remember that Hal is dead.

D-e-a-d.

At school, Ms. Leggly is teaching you to spell.

At home, no one is allowed to talk about Hal. All of his stuff is gone, even all the pictures of him, and every night when you get home from school, Mother is in her room saying her rosary and Patty brings a pot roast supper over. After she leaves, you help Helen with the dishes, and then you make sure Jacob brushes his teeth before he goes to bed. After that, you and Helen go to bed, too. When everyone is quiet, Mother comes out of her bedroom and goes to the pantry and gets a glass of wine to help her sleep and now, every night, Dad comes straight home from work without stopping for a beer and he eats three boiled beef sandwiches with horseradish and then they both go to bed.

You can never fall asleep first.

Sometimes when he thinks you are sleeping Dad comes in your room. Once he leaned over the top bunk and kissed your forehead. But you were only pretending to be asleep, and his horseradish breath made you sneeze.

He said, "You should be sleeping, kiddo."

After your writing lesson, you walk through the park. Even though you're not supposed to go there because they found a woman's body near the river. She was stabbed. It's dangerous by the river, Mother says, because hippies hang out by the bridge.

You are not afraid of hippies.

Even after Dad cut out the picture of the dead boy on the cover of TIME magazine and put it up on the refrigerator.

He said some hippies gave the boy a pill called LSD, and it made him think he could fly and he jumped out off the balcony of his apartment building and crushed all the bones in his body.

In the picture the boy looked like Hal, like he was sleeping.

You would tell Ms. Leggly if you found a body by the river, and she would call the police. She would believe you. Ms. Leggly has so many students in seventh grade that she stays after school to help kids who want help. She is the nicest teacher you have ever had. She is not a nun like Sister Francis, so she wears regular clothes. Every day she wears colorful scarves that match her springy red hair.

Today you told Ms. Leggly that you come everyday after school because you never want to have Sister Francis again. You don't mention the fact that if you got held back in seventh grade, then you and Helen would be in the same grade, and that would make you feel dumber than you already feel. You even confessed what kids call Sister Francis: Sister Francis of the Fat... but you spelled out the a-s-s part. You did not want to sin.

Ms. Leggly didn't even get mad. In fact, she sort of smiled. "May, darlin', you spelled that word right on the money, but you are pressing the life out of that poor pencil."

Ms. Leggly speaks very slowly. She is from the South and sounds a lot like Grandmother's maid, Bell, though her skin is super pale and she does not smell like bleach water. She smells like green apples, and she has a million freckles.

Today when you asked her if she knew the secret recipe for homemade Thousand Island dressing, she handed you a fresh piece of paper and said, "I haven't the foggiest notion, but why don't you write it out for me?"

Now you know how to spell relish.

R-e-l-i-s-h.

In the park you practice spelling *relish* in your head. You reach the bridge and there are no hippies, so you start across the wooden boards.

Halfway across the bridge, over the sound of rushing water, you hear sounds that are not coming from your feet. You look up and see the blind man walking straight toward you.

You've seen the blind man a million times before, sitting on his porch step with his dog outside his broken-down blue house next to the river. But you've never seen him out walking around by himself.

His dog never barks.

Helen says he is a mulatto. His skin is the color of cinnamon. He always wears thick dark glasses, and today, he is bundled up in an army jacket, with a bright orange hunting cap pulled down over his white hair.

When he hears you, he stops, and you stop, too.

You both just stand there for a while.

You listen to the sound of your own breathing.

You listen to the rush of the water.

His black dog is panting, and his red-tipped cane softly taps against the boards of the bridge floor. Yvonne said his dog is a German shepherd and it doesn't bark because he cut out its tongue. That's why she's not allowed to go down by the river, either.

The blind man's coat blocks your view of the dog's tongue. Even though it's not that cold out you start to shiver.

Your heart bumps against the inside of your chest and you try to hear what he is thinking, but you can't hear a thing.

The wind whips dry leaves across your feet and some of them blow off the edge of the bridge into the water below, where they float on their backs around the bend. A fine mist hangs in the air and makes you think of snow, but then the setting sun decides to peak out from behind a cloud and its warmth spreads across your cheek. And you know the blind man can feel it, too, because he turns his whole face toward the light and smiles. He calls out, "Feels good, don't it?"

You don't answer.

His head keeps wagging from side to side and he taps his red-tipped cane harder against the boards and you wonder if he is pretending to be blind so he can grab you.

Maybe he stabbed the woman down by the river.

Dad's words jump into your head. "Those folks would just as soon slit your throat as look at you."

But then, if he really is blind, maybe he doesn't even know what color he is.

A woman wearing a red hat comes up behind him walking her collie dog. She says, "Well, hello Albert," and the blind man smiles wide and wags his head and the two dogs sniff each other and the collie dog's tail wags so hard its hind end looks like it will fly off any second.

You try to walk by quickly, but the collie dog jumps at you whimpering and you have to stop. The woman pulls back on the leash and laughs, "He's friendly. You can pet him."

Then, before you know what's happening, you've taken off your mittens. And the blind man is pressing tiny biscuits from his pocket into your bare hand.

"They like these," he says, and he offers one to the German shepherd to show how to hold your hand flat. Like the blind man you put the biscuit in the middle so the dog can lick it off without biting any fingers and you offer the treat to the collie dog. His tongue tickles the palm of your hand.

You laugh.

"That's Rascal and my dog's Bo," the blind man says. His dog's ears perk up, but the collie dog just keeps panting. "What's your name?"

You're not supposed to talk to strangers. If Mother learned you were out here standing on the bridge, while it was getting dark, talking with a stranger in a red hat and a mulatto blind man, you would get in serious trouble. "Mmmmay," you stammer.

"May," the blind man repeats softly.

The bells of Sacred Heart begin to chime. "Goodness," the lady with the red hat exclaims, "only five, and it's getting dark."

You look around. Then, without saying good-bye, you bolt for home and the blind man calls after you, "I'll remember you, May."

And you run all the way, your heart is pounding and your feet feel like they are on fire and though you are not sure you believe in God anymore, you say a little prayer that Mother will never find out what you did. By the time your boots hit the back porch step the streetlights on Point Road are on and it is dark.

You push quietly through the back screen door onto the porch. Helen springs from the back door and startles you.

"Where's Mother?" you ask, automatically.

"Taking a nap. Dad went for pizza." Helen doesn't seem to notice you are late. She points at the floor. "You have to leave your shoes out here."

"Why?" You stuff your mittens into the sleeves of your jacket and kick off the red boots that protect your beat-up school shoes. Helen and Jacob's shoes are already lined up on a new rubber mat.

"It's a surprise!" Helen squeals and races back into the house.

Now that Helen has a friend, she seems happier, and even though you feel a little sad about her not wanting to walk with you, at least she is talking again.

"Is that May?" You hear Patty's voice coming from the living room as you open the porch door into the kitchen.

Patty is setting up TV trays for supper in the living room, because while you were at school, some workmen came and tore off the kitchen floor.

"It's like walking on sunflowers," Helen says, skidding around in her pink socks. "But it still needs to dry."

You look down at the new floor.

Helen is happy because next to pink, yellow is her second favorite color.

"Dad's bringing pizza!" Jacob announces from the hallway. He's holding a handful of Lincoln Logs and a massive Lincoln Log structure is blocking the walkway to the living room.

Patty steps over it and motions you into the living room, "It's okay to walk on it, honey."

But you just stand in the doorway and stare at the place where the blood spot used to be.

"Brrrr," Patty brushes her thick arms as she comes to greet you. "Let's close this door, it's letting the cold in," she says, hugging you into her warm round body.

"Come in and see the living room, too!" Helen grabs your hand and leads you through the kitchen just as Dad's car lights shine through the front window.

Jacob almost knocks both of you over trying to get back to help Dad with the pizza.

"Double pepperoni… double pepperoni…" he chants, racing by in his bare feet.

Helen shows off two new velvet blue chairs.

"We're not allowed to sit in them, but aren't they pretty?" she whispers.

After the pizza, Patty leaves and Dad goes to bed. You creep out into the kitchen to touch the place where the blood spot used to be. It feels cold and smooth like ice. Then Mother coughs behind her bedroom door and quietly, you hurry back to bed.

That night you dream about the blind man.

His head keeps wobbling all over the place and when you try to cross the bridge, he blocks your way. You get mad, "Did you murder the woman down by the river?" you ask.

He takes his glasses off and in his eye sockets are two yellow marbles and they split open like seeds and out of each one grows a giant sunflower and all he does is laugh and laugh and laugh.

When you wake up you still hear him laughing.

CHAPTER 16

The Happiest Day

ALL WINTER long you stay as far away from Promise Park as possible, except when you take Helen and Jacob over to Aunt Emma's house to go sledding. But you don't take them anywhere near the blind man's house.

Now you are glad the workmen came to put in the new kitchen floor that day. Nobody even noticed you were late, so you didn't get in any trouble.

For the Spring semester Ms. Leggly only meets with you on Mondays and Wednesdays after school. This is because your writing has progressed. Your reading, too. Ms. Leggly is *sooo* proud of you. She gave you a novel written by Harper Lee, *To Kill a Mockingbird*. Helen already read it, but you don't care.

"It'll probably take you a long time," she says every time she sees you reading it.

Even when she doesn't say it out loud, Helen still thinks you're stupid, but these days, you just ignore her, because

109

Ms. Leggly told you, "Darlin', don't believe anyone who says you aren't smart, because it's simply not true." On your report card she wrote: *May is one of the brightest students I've had the privilege to work with. Given that her vocabulary tested in the 98th percentile, her writing skills should follow. She is a hard worker who gives it her all.*

When you brought the report card home to show Mother, she said, "As long as you try your best, that's what counts," and she put down her rosary and got out of bed and pulled on her robe and came out into the kitchen and made real strawberry milkshakes for you and Helen and Jacob to celebrate.

It was the happiest day ever.

Lately, it seems like Mother is happier, though some days her arthritis acts up. Then she soaks her hands in a tub full of hot wax, and it's your job to dial the phone and call Dad at Titus, so he can take you and Helen and Jacob out for fried chicken.

You're great at memorizing numbers.

It's just how your brain works.

258-3469, that's the number for Titus Tannery.

It's easy to remember because it adds up to 37, which is a prime number, which means it can't be divided by anything except itself. It's also exactly 2 years older than what Mother turned on her last birthday, which was 35, and if you divide 35 by 2, you get 17.5, which is the exact number of months that Hal has been dead. You are not sure what that means but you suspect it means something. Why else would it circle around in your brain?

Even though Mother is getting older, she still gets nervous, especially if she feels like all you kids are getting in her hair, but luckily, she doesn't spank much anymore. Not since the day of the accident.

Helen says, "It's because her hands hurt."

Jacob says, "It's because her wooden spoons are all broken."

You think it has something to do with Hal being gone and the fact that she only has three children left and she's decided to be nicer to you all. Even when she does get mad, you know she loves you, because she still does nice things, sometimes. She's learning to knit so she can exercise her fingers, and she made you a blue scarf and Helen a pink one and Jacob an orange one. Those are everyone's favorite colors.

Today, you were planning to wear your scarf all day at school. But Ms. Leggly made you put it away so it wouldn't get paint on it.

Ms. Leggly's entire classroom is being converted into a jungle. She wants to teach the kids at Sacred Heart about Africa and slavery and civil rights, because this year two black families moved into Pig Valley. They are sending their kids to Sacred Heart. One boy is in Jacob's grade and he looks like Michael Jackson of the Jackson Five, but Jacob says it's not him. It's a paper jungle, but it almost looks real. Ms. Leggly put you and Yvonne in charge of painting the monkeys, but Yvonne's monkey looks more like a gorilla, because she modeled him after Sampson.

Sampson lives at the County Zoo.

He's lived there more than twice as long as you've been alive.

Sampson came from Africa and he has the saddest eyes a person ever saw.

Thinking of Sampson makes you feel sad, sad, sad.

As you put away paints you try not to think about him, or his eyes, because you hate feeling sad. When you feel sad, it makes you think of Hal, and when you think of Hal, it makes you want to cry, but you can't cry because Yvonne would see, and Dad is counting on you. These days Dad says he doesn't know what he would do without you.

You are his rock.

Yvonne thinks Sampson wants to die. Putting the little tubes of paint in their proper place you decide maybe she is right. When Ms. Leggly took your class to the zoo, she let you and Yvonne wait by yourselves in the monkey house while the rest of the class finished up in the reptile house and Yvonne banged on the glass to make Sampson look at her. He just sat there staring straight ahead with those eyes. When the rest of the class came in and banged on the glass and waved their hands and their hats and yelled at him to make him get up or move or do something, Ms. Leggly made them stop. It didn't matter. Sampson just sat there staring at the yellow tile floor like he didn't care about a thing.

Or if he was dead or alive.

"He misses his dad," Yvonne said on the bus on the way home. "That's why he wants to die."

You close your eyes and shake your head to try to forget poor Sampson. Then you open your eyes and carefully reread the labels on the shelves to make sure you put everything away right. The way Ms. Leggly likes it. You don't want to make any mistakes. Ms. Leggly is counting on you. It makes some sense to you that Sampson would have a dad and a mother, but does he have brothers and sisters, too? And does he still think about them? Do they think about him? Perhaps so much time has passed, none of them can remember each other.

You check the paint tubes one more time and try to remember Hal.

All you can remember is the leprechauns.

They were different colors like the paint tubes:

Red.

Orange.

Yellow.

Green.

Blue.

Purple.

Violet.

Why it is getting harder and harder to remember Hal?

If only you had just one picture of him, to remind you he was real. Then you try to remember if Sampson had blue eyes like Yvonne painted them, but you think they were green like yours and Hal's. Hard as you try, you can't remember Hal's eyes at all, and deep inside you feel tons of tears backing up in your brain, wanting to come out.

But they don't.

CHAPTER 17

The Trip

STANDING ON the back porch, you reach down to take off your shoes when Helen and Jacob rush at you through the back door smiling.

"Guess what?" Helen says.

"We're going to New Jersey!" Jacob blurts.

"Do you have to ruin everything?" Helen elbows him hard.

Jacob ducks out of the way. "To see Grandmother Golding for Easter!" he sings, sliding down onto his knees and skidding across the shiny yellow linoleum.

"Today?" You look at Helen.

She nods.

"We get to miss school?"

Helen nods again.

"Dad's going to drive while we sleep," Jacob practically shouts.

Helen spins around. "SHUT UP—stupid."

"No—I can say what I want." Jacob drops to his knees and, crawling across the kitchen floor, starts barking at Helen.

"Don't call him stupid," you say to Helen and give Jacob a long look. "Shush, Mother is sleeping."

"She's not. And you are not the boss of me, and he *is* stupid. Look at him." Helen stares at Jacob with disgust.

Jacob barks at her some more, then crawls over near her feet and lifts his back leg like he is going to pee.

"Stop!" She grabs his ear like she is going to rip it off of his head and you jump in trying to separate them, but Helen cries out hysterically and starts flailing and screaming, "Make him stop! I hate him. Why... why... why couldn't *he* have died instead of HAL?"

Jacob stops.

You drop her arm.

Both of you look at her, and then she spits right in your face and runs for the bathroom and the bathroom door slams shut and the lock clicks and neither you nor Jacob move—

It's like someone has frozen you.

The warm wet spit runs down your cheek.

Helen's words bounce around in your brain, and you're not sure what to do, but after a million years you finally wipe the spit off your face and ask, "Where's Mother?"

Jacob shrugs. "I think she's in the basement getting the suitcases."

"Is Dad coming home early?"

Jacob nods.

He leans back thoughtfully on his knees.

"May, do you wish I was dead?"

"No."

"If we were both dead, we could play with Hal, and Helen wouldn't get to see him."

You start to say he's probably got other work to do now that he's an angel, but you stop yourself.

"May, I'm not stupid, am I?"

"Helen thinks everyone is stupid except her."

"Yeah, she's the one who's stupid," Jacob agrees.

His hair is cut just like Dad's and you pat his bristly head like he really is a dog. He makes a whimpering sound. You laugh and pet him more and he rolls over onto his back and you start to tickle his belly and he tries to tickle yours and soon both of you are laughing so hard you have to stop to catch your breath. Helen comes out of the bathroom and says in a sort-of-nice voice, "You guys better stop goofing around and get packed or Mother will hear and get mad."

Mother does hear, because her voice booms up from the bottom of the stairs, "May? Is that you? Come help with these."

And you race down the steps, where, to your amazement, Mother is dressed in regular clothes. You help her lug the suitcases up one at a time.

"I can do it, Mother. Don't hurt your hands." You boss her around just a little bit so that she'll let you do it.

The next morning you wake up in New Jersey. You can't remember getting from the car to the bed in Grandmother's guest room. But you like waking up at Grandmother's house tucked into the softest sheets in the world with the smell of Dove soap everywhere. Two tall windows are open, because Dad complains about Grandmother keeping the house as hot as a steam bath. The white lace curtains are billowing out in the breeze and Helen is asleep in the twin bed next to you, and Jacob is on a cot at the end of your bed. Mother and Dad are still asleep in the adjacent guest room because they probably stayed up drinking wine with Grandmother.

Sometimes you wonder why you always fall asleep last and wake up first, but this morning you are glad for it, because you can just lie there and let the softness of Grandmother's house seep into your bones.

No one talks about Grandmother being rich, but she is.

Her house is huge. It has its own library, which is where you and Helen and Jacob end up spending most of the day because outside it is too damp and Grandmother wants to help keep you kids out of Mother's hair.

Grandmother takes naps too, but before she goes to her room, she teaches you how to play a card game called Russian Banks. It takes two decks of cards. She teaches Jacob first, then Helen, then all three of you beat her, one game at a time, though you suspect she lost on purpose.

After she goes up for her nap, you and Jacob play Go Fish, because Helen says, "Card games are stupid," and you are having a hard time remembering all the rules for Russian Banks.

"Go Fish is the stupidest game in the world," Helen says, not looking up from a book about birds of North America.

You and Jacob ignore her.

Just before dinner Aunt Cleo calls to wish everyone a happy Easter. She couldn't come to New Jersey because they are short on staff at the country club where she works. She can't be a waitress because of only having one arm, so they need her to hostess, which is her favorite part. She promised to call again when her shift is over.

Dad tells you and Helen and Jacob to go wake Mother and change into your church clothes for supper. You let Jacob knock on Mother's door. "The roast lamb is almost ready," he hollers through the door, and you immediately shush him, but Mother's voice comes from the other side. "It's all right, May. I'll be down shortly."

You are relieved that her voice sounds calm and nice, like when she is feeling happy, or if she's had a glass of wine.

Helen and Jacob take forever to change, so you jump into a church dress and your new leather loafers and race back downstairs, where Dad and Grandmother are in the kitchen picking up where Bell left off.

Bell did not have to work today because it is the weekend, but she set the dining room table with the good crystal and china and silver, and she made most of the food ahead of time so that it would be ready to put on the table.

Grandmother doesn't cook.

Grandmother has always had maids.

She doesn't understand why her son married Mother, because Mother is Irish and though she went to college and she is very smart, she is not rich. Once, Grandmother confessed she likes all of you, anyway, and what's done is done.

"Go fill up those water goblets," Dad says, handing you a sweating silver pitcher of water.

Grandmother is carving the roast lamb with a pearl-handled carving knife. The chunk of meat is so juicy that its blood spills out into the little rivulets of the silver platter and a part of you just wants to watch, but Dad says, "Go on, May."

So you tear yourself away and go into the dining room where there are six lit candelabras and more steaming food: a silver bowl of green beans and an identical bowl of mashed potatoes with little pads of golden butter melting all over it, and a basket full of bread and fresh muffins, and two delicate blue crystal bowls filled with mint jelly, each with its own matching tiny silver spoon. And there are finger bowls with lemon slices and parsley, and pressed linen napkins in monogrammed silver napkin rings. And coffee cups and bowls of cubed sugar with silver tongs and individual crystal creamers and china bowls filled with green salad and Bell's homemade Thousand Island dressing in a small crystal decanter for the kids.

It is the most amazing table you have ever seen.

So beautiful it almost takes your breath away.

Then you spot the lamb cake with pink jelly bean eyes. It's covered with coconut frosting and resting on a bed of green Easter grass right in front of Grandmother's place, and you don't know why, but you just have to sit down by that cake. You have never seen a cake shaped liked a real animal. And you have always loved lambs. You remember the time Aunt Cleo brought you to the petting zoo and you fed a real lamb. It had the softest nose in the world. Then you can't help yourself, you put down the pitcher and touch the lamb's nose, but it is not anything like the real lamb, and a blob of frosting gets on your finger and you quickly lick it off as Helen and Jacob come bounding through the swinging door.

"I'm telling!" Helen cries.

You pick up a crystal goblet and start pouring water again, licking at the sugar on your lips. "I didn't do anything."

"May tasted the lamb cake!" Helen yells loud enough for everyone to hear.

"Stay away from the food," Dad yells from the kitchen.

Jacob races up to the edge of the table and stares at the lamb cake. His bow tie is on crooked. "Cool," he says.

Mother comes into the dining room holding a corkscrew and a bottle of wine. She is trying to open it. Her face is twisted up and tight. Perhaps her hands are hurting again.

"I can do it," you offer, but she doesn't seem to know that you are there. So, you finish filling the goblets and edge over to the clawfooted chair down by the lamb cake before Helen and Jacob think of it.

"Fix your tie," Mother snarls at Jacob. She cranks down on the corkscrew. "This damn thing."

When Mother swears it is never a good sign.

"Can I sit near the lamb cake?" Helen asks.

In the kitchen you hear Grandmother yell something about gravy and there is a sound of slamming dishes. She doesn't know how to make the gravy, and neither does Dad.

"Oh, for God's sake," Mother says under her breath and she cranks on the wine bottle again.

When you are strategically in front of the chair you want, you put down the pitcher, fix Jacob's tie, and slowly edge the clawfooted chair away from the table.

Suddenly, Helen stomps her foot and screams, "This is my place. I got here first!"

Mother doesn't even look up and you know that no one can sit down until Grandmother comes into the room and that you are stronger than Helen and for some reason you just have to sit by the lamb cake, so you push against her with your body and she flops down crying on the floor and makes such a racket Mother looks up.

"May knocked me down! I want to sit by Grandmother this time. It's my turn."

Mother's eyes get a frantic look. She shakes her head. "For Christ sake, stop your nonsense."

The yelling in the kitchen gets louder.

Then everything goes into slow motion: Mother twists harder and harder on the cork screw, and you know it would work better if she set the bottle down on the table like a stuck paint tube and you see the tears well up in her eyes and you forget about Helen and the lamb cake and the chair and go to try to help, but as you reach for the bottle she raises it up into the air and everything happens so fast as the bottle

       slams

           into

              your

                  face.

CHAPTER 18

The Talk

WHEN THE bottle crash lands there is a loud crack and your head ricochets against Grandmother's white stucco wall and blood splatters everywhere. Onto the wall. Onto the oriental rug. Onto Helen, who screams, but you don't make a sound because you don't feel anything, except an explosion of heat near your nose.

Your face feels…

Hot.

When you open your eyes, you are on the floor, and there's blood dripping down the front of your church dress and Mother drops the bottle, which never did open, and it rolls into the corner. She grabs the front of your dress and yanks you to your feet.

"Don't get blood on the oriental carpet!"

You blink, everything is blurry, and your mouth tastes like metal and salt, and you put a hand up to try to catch the stream gushing from your nose but it spills onto the rug anyway, and when you can't stop the blood from getting all over, your legs start to shake, like they do when she's got a wooden spoon, and you try to keep standing, but your legs buckle and you sink slowly back down to the floor.

Mother doesn't pull you up again, she just stands there, staring down at you, wringing her blood-smeared hands. It's like they are hurt and she doesn't know what to do.

Helen closes her eyes and covers her ears.

Jacob makes a siren sound.

Dad rushes into the dining room and picks you up off the floor. "Calm down! Now, everybody calm down," he shouts, and Grandmother, who has followed behind him, says, "Oh my, that's a lot of blood. I'll get ice," and she rushes back into the kitchen.

Through the blurriness you see Dad looking at the mess and his worry washes over you like fast-running river water. He helps you into Grandmother's bedroom, and you hear him thinking about Hal and this makes you think about Hal, too.

Hal died from a cracked head.

You heard Aunt Cleo tell someone that Hal had a gash on his forehead, and he died of head and internal injuries. If he'd lived, he'd have been a vegetable.

Maybe it's better he died.

Maybe you'll die, too.

Then you can be with him.

Dad carefully leads you to Grandmother's bed. He takes a book of matches out of his back pocket and rips the cardboard cover off and folds it three times.

"Keep your head forward, dear," Grandmother coos, coming into the room with a silver bucket and an ice pack. She hands Dad a cold damp washcloth and he wipes some of the blood away from your face. Instinctively you tilt your head back, so the blood doesn't drip all over the place, but the blood begins running down the back of your throat and you cough. Dad catches what comes out with the washcloth.

"Keep your head pitched forward." Grandmother's voice is firm, but calm. "Otherwise you'll choke."

You do as she says.

Dad hands you the little piece of folded matchbook cover. "Put this under your top lip, keep pressure on. It'll help stop the bleeding." He slides the little piece of cardboard in place. Your mouth tastes of blood and sulfur and something that reminds you of shaving cream.

You do as he says.

"I'll finish up. You'd better go out there and attend to *her*, before anything else happens," Grandmother says to Dad. She presses the blue ice pack up to the side of your face. The look she gives him means more than she is saying.

Dad does as he's told.

"Hold it like this, dear." Grandmother is pressing too hard and the ice feels so cold the hot, hot, hot feeling comes back so you pull it away a little, which she doesn't seem to mind. Finally, she lets you hold it and she goes over to her dresser and pulls out a silver monogrammed sewing kit and one of her own peach-colored silk night gowns. "The dress is ruined, so we might as well make you comfortable."

She sets the silk nightgown on the end of the bed and pulls out a small silver scissors shaped like an exotic bird. Carefully she cuts the dress and the soiled slip right off your body.

The scissors feel cold against your skin.

"No, Muutthermmmightgetmmmad," you try to say.

"Don't try to talk, dear, you'll swallow more blood," she says, noticing the goosebumps jumping up on your body. She puts her fingers between your skin and the scissors and expertly continues cutting.

Secretly, you decide, if Mother does get mad about the stupid dress, you'll tell her it was her fault. Though you know in real life you would never talk back.

Strip by strip, Grandmother peels the dress from your body. More and more bare skin shivers in the cool air of the bedroom.

"Lean forward, May."

You start to shiver all over.

"May, you are getting so tall, I never noticed until now," Grandmother says softly, more to herself than you.

Your mouth tastes like you've been licking the brewery fence at home and all the blood running down the back of your throat is making you feel queasy, but the throbbing in your nose keeps you from thinking about throwing up. You don't want to think about it because you hate throwing up.

When you are finally cleaned up and settled into one of grandmother's silk nightgowns, she tucks the soft pile of cotton blankets around you and says, "I'll be back to check on you after dinner. You keep that ice on. It's starting to slow a bit."

Then she looks at you.

She has blue eyes like Helen and Jacob and Dad.

She sets a bucket beside you on the bed.

"Try not to swallow the blood, dear."

You nod just the little tiniest bit. Before she leaves, she switches on the radio by the side of the bed. The soft hum of a Gregorian chant fills the room. It is so much better than the silence and it helps you not to think about being alone in Grandmother's fancy electric bed that moves up and down with the touch of a button, or that you are holding a freezing blue ice pack to your nose, while everyone else is in the dining room eating Easter dinner.

A few minutes later, above the sounds on the radio, you hear the murmur of everyone saying grace, and then the sound of knives and forks scratching across the dinner plates. Every few minutes your mouth fills up with blood and you spit into the silver bucket.

After the Gregorian chant ends, an organ song comes on.

You hate organ songs.

They remind you of churches, which remind you of God, who reminds you of Hal. Now Hal is an angel up in heaven with God, even though God hardly gave him a chance to live, so you try to block out the organ music in your brain, but then your brain starts thinking about the lamb cake, and about Helen sitting in the claw-footed mahogany chair right in front of the lamb cake, chewing on a juicy piece of meat.

You can't help it.

You wonder what the lamb cake tastes like.

Does it have layers, like a regular cake? Is it filled with something good, like banana pudding, or whip cream frosting? Perhap there are sprinkles inside, like the Fourth of July cake that Aunt Emma made last summer for the fireworks picnic.

Normally your stomach would be growling, but it starts to feel weird and whirly. The lamb cake with its coconut frosting takes over your brain, and even with blood in your mouth, you can taste the coconut frosting. It reminds you of the Novaks and potato pancakes and Neopolitan candy, which you ate instead of telling Mr. Novak that you forgave him for killing Hal.

And then… you suddenly remember.

You hate coconut.

It tastes like grass!

And this makes your mouth go dry and while you're busy reminding yourself that you're not missing out on anything, you hear Helen whisper.

"May?"

She peeks around the door into Grandmother's room.

You look over and try to say something, but your lips are swollen shut. They feel bumped out, and you know they look bad because Helen stares at them as she comes up beside the bed.

"I said I had to go to the bathroom," she says quietly.

You nod. A part of you feels grateful.

"Does it hurt?"

You nod.

"Mother went back to bed." Helen looks down into the bucket filled with blood. She gags and looks away.

"Grandmother gave her a pill."

You're not sure how you feel about this news. Some pills make Mother sleepy, but some make her go crazy, like with the wine bottle.

"Helen?" Grandmother's voice comes from the dining room.

"I'm coming," Helen calls back. She leans near your ear and whispers, "I made sure no one sat in your place."

"Helen! Don't be in there bothering your sister, she needs rest." Grandmother's heels come clicking down the hall. Helen turns and races back to the door. Your stiff lips smile, even though it hurts a little, because Helen doesn't hate you anymore.

Like before Hal died.

"I'll attend to May." Grandmother puts her hand on Helen's shoulder. "You help your father clear the dishes."

They are standing just outside the bedroom door.

"I'll save you lamb cake," Helen says before she runs off.

You try to yell after her, "Thaaanks," but the little piece of cardboard falls out onto your lap and Grandmother says, "No talking." She puts her finger to her lips and sits next to you on the edge of the bed. She gently pulls the ice pack away from your face. A freezing drop of water slides down on your shoulder and you quiver.

"Oh my, oh my!" Grandmother exclaims shaking her head and fussing with the blankets. She tilts your chin back to examine your nose, which does seem to have stopped bleeding, but a big gulp of blood slides down your throat and you cough and she lets go and wraps her arms around you.

"Oh my, oh my," she coos.

You close your eyes, because in your family people don't usually touch each other.

You don't know why.

But mostly you like it.

It feels strange and makes you feel stiff and only a little scared, and despite your nose being smashed to pieces, you smell her Dove soap and remember that she has never hit anyone you know of, so you keep your eyes shut and rest, until Dad walks in the room.

"Has it stopped?"

"It's slowed down," Grandmother says.

"Her dinner's on the counter." He talks like you are not even there.

You open your eyes, but you don't feel very hungry.

"Maybe we should take her into Memorial. Get it cauterized," Grandmother suggests. She pulls the pillow up behind your back.

What does *cauterized* mean? You don't like the sound of it. And Memorial is where your Grandfather worked when he was alive. You wish he still was alive, because he was a doctor, and he could tell if you had a cracked head, and if it needed to get *cauterized*.

Your brain starts to try to spell the word *cauterized*, C- a- w- t- e- r- e- y -e- s.

Dad notices the bloody matchbook cover in your lap. He picks it up and hands it back to you. "Keep pressing this under your lip, May. It'll work."

You stop trying to spell and try not to feel how slippery and slimy the cardboard feels in your fingers.

He leaves the room.

Grandmother follows him.

"What if it's broken?"

"It's not broken," he replies.

Grandmother closes the door. "How do you know?"

"Her eyes aren't dilated."

Grandmother's voice shoots up an octave. "That doesn't mean anything." She adds, "They probably covered concussions after you flunked out of medical school."

"Mother, that's enough. If it doesn't stop we'll take her in."

"I think we should take her in now!"

There's a long pause, and Dad sighs, "And tell them *what*?" By the tone of his voice he is angry.

Outside of the door Grandmother doesn't make a peep.

"I mean, don't you think this family has been through enough?"

"We need to make sure—

"It's better for everyone if we just deal with this on our own."

The knob turns a little on the door.

"Fine. You take care of the others. I'll sit with her."

You hear Dad's voice fade down the hallway, "Helen, Jacob, no more TV. Time for bed."

"Aw, Aunt Cleo said we could stay up and talk with her on the phone after her shift," Jacob complains. You hear his feet bouncing around on the tile floor.

"She'll call again in the morning."

"Tell Jacob," Helen says, disgusted, "to stop hopping like a rabbit!"

"Jacob—stop hopping like a rabbit," Dad imitates Helen. Then he and Jacob start laughing.

"It's not funny," Helen whines.

Grandmother lets herself back into the room.

She pulls a sitting chair up by the side of the bed. She picks up her embroidery basket and sets it in her lap and looks over at you. Even though she's acting all strong and calm, you know she's not. Her blue eyes look worried, so you study the spot directly above her eyebrows. They are two perfect brown arches that she paints on with an eyebrow pencil every morning. She shaved her real eyebrows off with a razor because she didn't like the way they looked.

"May?" she says.

Should you answer?

She holds up an embroidery needle. "I want to have a talk with you... explain a few things... you're old enough to understand... about your mother."

Despite the folded matchbook cover, the words, "I jjjjust wannnted to helppp—" force themselves out.

Grandmother pats your knee.

"I know, dear. I know."

She looks down at her embroidery. She's making a pillowcase with roses on it and you remember the smell of Locker's Greenhouse and O'Leary's Funeral Home, and you start thinking about cracked heads. Did the wine bottle crack your head bad enough to die?

You know this is what Grandmother is worried about. For some reason, she doesn't say so. Why does everyone in your family pretend like everything is all right?

They took Hal to the hospital and now he's dead.

It's your fault.

You left him.

You're getting what you deserve, a cracked head.

"Why does Mother go crazy?" you ask, taking the piece of cardboard out from under your lip because you're suddenly sick and tired of holding it there.

Grandmother looks you straight in the eye. "Dear, your mother is like a fine horse. No one really knows what might spook her. It's the way it is, whether we like it or not."

"This is the worst Easter of my life," you say.

Grandmother looks back down at her embroidery. Then back at you. "I would imagine it is," she says sadly.

A drop of blood drips onto your hand.

You lick it off.

She shakes her head. She doesn't say what she's thinking. Which is how she should take all of you kids somewhere without Mother, and you want to tell her that you'd like that a lot. Helen would, too. But you don't say anything, because then she'll know you know what she's thinking. So, instead, you shove the matchbook cover back in place and turn away from her.

You close your eyes, because you can't stand to look at her, she looks too much like Dad, who's counting on you to help when Mother goes crazy.

All night long wild horses stampede through your dreams and when you wake up only one of your eyes wants to open. The other is crusted over with dried blood. Someone put a towel under your head and you are back in the twin bed, in Grandmother's front room, and it feels like your body has turned into the Tin Man's body and it needs a ton of oil, so you try not to move.

Helen and Jacob are still asleep, so you just lie there and wait. Even though Grandmother's sheets feel soft, you start to wish you had a different family, like Helen always does. A family where the mother doesn't go crazy and the dad listens when you know things. But is wishing for a different family some kind of sin? You start to think about Sampson. How he sits all by himself in the big yellow-tiled cage, how his family probably does not even remember him anymore. This makes you think of Hal and you wonder if Hal can hear you, the way you can sometimes hear people thinking, and if he knows that maybe it's good he's dead because Mother still goes crazy, and then a part of you starts to wish you were dead, so you could be with him, instead of with the rest of your family.

Except, maybe Aunt Cleo. You know if Aunt Cleo saw your mashed nose and puffy lip, she would ask what happened.

If Aunt Cleo were here, you would tell her.

Everything.

CHAPTER 19

The News

IT TAKES Grandmother over a year to organize another vacation without Mother and Dad. But she does it. When she calls, she tells Dad she'd like to get you kids out of Mother's hair for a while, so Mother can rest, and she's arranged for all of you to spend the summer with her at a cottage up on Lake Superior. It's where she spent her summers as a child, a place in northern Wisconsin where people go to get out of the humidity for a while.

At dinner, when Dad announces this news, Helen looks worried.

"Don't you want to go?" Dad asks, plopping a spoonful of reconstituted potato flakes onto her plate.

Mother has been making the same dinner almost every night and Dad makes everyone say how much they like it. Broiled beef, instant potato flakes, and frozen vegetables, with your least favorite food in the entire world—lima beans!

"Not so much," Helen whines.

Dad ignores her. "Why don't you want to go?"

"Can Marie come?"

"No, honey, this is just for family."

Helen frowns and mucks her fork around in the potatoes.

She and Marie have sworn to be best friends forever. They do everything together, even though this year Marie got bumped up into your eighth grade class at Sacred Heart because she was so smart. You like Marie, too, but Helen says you are not allowed to be friends with her because she was Helen's friend first. Marie is nice to you anyway, and secretly she helped with your end-of-the-year spelling tests, so that you'd graduate from Sacred Heart.

You still don't get A's like Helen and Jacob. But now you get B's in almost every class.

"Just us?" Jacob scrunches up his face.

Dad and Mother both nod.

"Just the kids." Mother smiles at Jacob and gives him some of the meat off of her plate, because even though he's only nine, he eats almost as much as Dad.

"Your cousins will be there, too, at least for part of the time." She yanks off a big chunk of fatty gristle and tosses it onto Dad's plate.

"Ewwoooe!" both you and Helen exclaim.

Dad smiles.

He loves fat and gristle.

He stabs the wobbly glob with a fork and gobbles it up and then smiles at Mother with greasy lips. You look across the table at Helen and grimace, and all the while Dad and

Mother keep smiling at one another. They seem happier lately, since Dad got a new job and summer is here and Mother has started doing all sorts of projects, like painting the porch and planting petunias.

She even looks different, only you can't figure out why.

Maybe it's because when you got home Dad moved all of the wine and beer bottles to the basement cellar and he locked them up so that only he has the key. You are glad they're down there. It helps you to forget what happened. Once in a while, when your nose still bleeds for no reason, you remember, but that only happens at night. It makes a mess, but it doesn't hurt.

Just in case, Dad gave you a bunch of matchbook covers to keep under your pillow.

"Does the cottage have a beach?" Jacob asks, his mouth full of meat.

"Don't talk with your mouth full," Dad says.

"A nice one with white sand," Mother says.

You don't say anything, because already your brain is switching into overdrive and you wonder how Grandmother will possibly take care of all those children by herself, but Dad answers this before you can ask.

"She's hired a sitter, and she's a lifeguard, and she'll take you to the beach every day and your Aunt Cleo will be there, too."

This makes your heart happy. Aunt Cleo likes to read books and she has promised to read you her all-time favorite: *The Secret Garden*.

"Is she fat like Patty?" Jacob asks.

"Is who fat?" Dad laughs.

"The babysitter."

Mother smiles and Dad smiles back at her.

"Jacob, that is not polite. I'm sure she will be a very nice person."

"Patty is not fat!" Helen comes to Patty's defense.

"Is too!"

"Is not."

While everyone is arguing, you pour applesauce over the mixed vegetables. Lima beans taste like chalk, so you've learned how to swallow them whole, like a pill, inside of a big glop of applesauce, because Dad makes you eat every single one of them. Luckily, since your nose got smashed, you can't smell much anymore. This helps a lot, because if you had to smell the lima beans, you doubt you could even swallow them.

"Is too. Is too. Is too!" Jacob sneers at Helen across the table.

"All right, that's enough you two." Dad waves his fork in the air, but Jacob is on a roll. He spreads out his arms. "You have to hug her like this," he giggles, and looks at Mother, like he knows a secret. "And now we have to hug Mother like that, because she's getting fat, too!" He waves his arms around excitedly.

You and Helen stare at him, astonished. You look at Mother. Telling Mother she's getting fat probably isn't a good idea, but Mother laughs.

Dad starts laughing, too.

You and Helen look at one another. Something very very strange is going on.

Mother pushes her chair away from the table and stands up. For the first time you notice how round her belly has gotten. Dad reaches over and rubs Jacob's bristly crewcut.

"No secrets in this house, huh?"

"Mother's getting fat and only I know why!" Jacob sings out.

"A baby?" Helen whispers. She doesn't spell it, but you do, in your head, *b-a-b-y*.

Ever since Ms. Leggly and Marie began helping you spell words, your head has started to spell words by itself. It's as if there is someone else talking inside of your brain.

Mother smiles and nods.

So does Dad.

"Jacob guessed it this morning." Mother pats Jacob's head.

Jacob takes a gulp of milk, puts down his glass, and wipes his mouth with the back of his hand. "It's a boy."

"You don't even know." She doesn't call him stupid.

"It's a boy. It's a boy. It's a boy...." Jacob taunts, and Helen squeezes her fork so hard it bends in her hands and she bursts into tears and runs back to her bottom bunk. Through the thin kitchen walls, you hear her body thud down on the mattress.

Jacob laughs.

"Jacob—" you say, but Dad puts his finger to his lips to stop you.

"Enough."

Dad gives Jacob a look. He stops, too.

"If I had a dollar for every time that kid cried, we'd be millionaires," says Dad. "Now, listen, you'll all have a wonderful time with your Grandmother and when you get home you will have a new brother *or* sister."

"It's a boy," Jacob whispers under his breath.

You help with the dishes and then go back to your bedroom to see how Helen is doing, but she is asleep under a pink blanket, so you skip brushing your teeth, pull off your socks and without bothering with pajamas you quietly climb up into the top bunk.

That night, you hear Dad and Mother laughing in the living room. Aunt Emma has stopped by to drop off homemade corned beef and cabbage, Dad's favorite. They are telling her the story of how Jacob guessed about the baby.

Long after she leaves and they've gone to bed, you are still awake.

Since the wine bottle incident, you have to sleep on your right side facing the door. If you don't, your nose plugs up or starts to bleed and you wake up choking for air. You could die, and you are afraid to die in the nighttime, because if Helen woke up and found you dead she would never stop crying.

Sometimes you worry Helen cries too much.

Even though she says she hates this family, and she told Jacob she wished he was dead, you know she doesn't really want anyone else dead. And now, even though Helen would rather have a baby sister, you know Jacob is right—it's a boy.

A baby boy.

What if Jacob has been right all along?

Has God, somehow, shrunk Hal down and put him back in Mother's stomach? But how could this possibly be true?

Why would God make it happen this way? And make everyone all sad and have a funeral and bury Hal's body in the freezing dirt? And let you lie awake at night wondering if you will ever see him again and then, suddenly, bring him back as a new baby?

You just can't understand.

But you do know one thing: it's a boy.

You decide not to say anything right away. It might make Helen cry more. Even if she asks, you'll wait.

Maybe you'll tell her when you're already at the cottage with Grandmother and your cousins.

Maybe.

CHAPTER 20

The Cottage

THE COTTAGE turns out to be more like a mansion made out of logs. It has a dozen bedrooms and a separate little cabin that used to be the maid's quarters. And a huge screen porch with porch swings and rattan chairs and little tables painted with daisies you can set your ice teas on. In the great room there is a huge ceiling fan. It looks like the propeller of the biggest plane ever made, and there is a real fireplace. Off of the kitchen there is a dining room with a long long table. It's not as fancy as Grandmother's house, but for a summer house, it's just as grand.

Outside of the log house a green lawn slopes down to the lake and the only neighbor lives in a huge white house on a distant cliff. Between the houses there are rows and rows of towering pine trees. You are so glad part of your nose still works because you have never smelled or felt air like this before.

It feels like it goes right through your skin and into your body.

Into your bones.

Grandmother calls it sea air. You decide Lake Superior looks just as big as Lake Michigan. But since you're not in the city with skyscrapers all around, you like it better.

Dad waves good-bye from the window of his new red Cadillac, the car he got for his new job. You stand beside Grandmother and feel the wind from the lake pushing against your back. It feels like it's playing tag with you, begging you to turn around and run toward it, toward the waves and the bluffs and the cliffs and the deep green smell of the water.

As the Cadillac disappears down the gravel drive, Helen starts to cry. Grandmother takes her hand. "Oh my, my, he'll be back here before you know it."

"Can we go by the water?" Jacob starts jumping up and down. "Can we? Can we?"

Grandmother hugs Helen. "When Lynn gets here, she'll take you to the beach. What do you think about that?"

She's trying to cheer Helen up. But Helen just sobs louder.

You put your arm around Jacob, because his jumping is making Helen even more agitated and though you want to go down to the water, too, you start rubbing his back.

He points at the shadowy outline of a distant ship, "Look, there's a freighter."

Squinting into the horizon, you nod.

"It looks small but it's really big," Jacob says matter-of-factly, looking up at you. He adds, "It's probably carrying coal."

Helen peeks her head out from Grandmother's arms. She wants to say something to Jacob, but she doesn't. Grandmother looks out at the freighter, too.

Helen whimpers quietly.

"All of your cousins will get here soon. Then you can play in the water or go down to the clubhouse or take a hike in the woods, whatever you'd like." Seeing that she is having some effect, she says, "And on Sunday we'll call your Mother and Dad and tell them how much fun you're having."

Helen sucks in a breath.

"Please don't cry, darling," Grandmother says. Helen actually stops.

You hear tires on the gravel drive and wonder if Dad forgot something, but it's a green jeep with no top on it and it pulls up and stops in front of the maid's quarters. Out jumps a grown-up girl with long blond hair tied back in a bright sky-blue kerchief. She's wearing sandals and sunglasses, so you can't see her eyes.

"Is that Lynn?" Helen wipes her face.

Grandmother nods. She calls out, "Lynn come and meet our first arrivals."

Lynn takes off her sunglasses and strolls toward you with an easy gait.

"Hi," she says shyly.

And then she quickly takes off the kerchief, shakes out her long blond hair, folds up the kerchief and sticks it in the back pocket of her jean shorts.

"Will you take us down by the water? Grandmother said you would." Jacob looks up at Grandmother, who laughs, and says, "Let's let the poor girl get settled in first."

You and Jacob carry up her two large green duffle bags. Helen lopes along behind looking sad, though she seems curious about Lynn. And then, by holding her hand on the way to the beach, Lynn completely wins Helen over.

Helen loves holding hands with strangers.

She holds hands with Marie back home, too.

Yvonne never holds your hand, but it doesn't matter because when anyone holds your hand it's usually because you are helping someone cross the street or something, and it'd feel funny to hold hands for no reason at all.

Lynn and Helen lead the way to the beach.

There is a winding steep sandy path, and the closer you get to the water, the more the wind tries to knock you over. Lynn kicks off her sandals and says you and Helen and Jacob should take off your shoes because they'll get wet.

Lynn flaps her wings like a bird and then takes off running down the long sand beach. You all follow her, flapping your wings too.

Up and down.

The waves wash in and out and spew up spray that makes your hair and your skin and your clothes smell like the water. The wet sand and the water feel freezing cold, but the dry sand is so hot it burns the bottom of your feet. Lynn shows you how to wait for the waves and chase after the small shells and pieces of glass that keep washing up at the edge of the foaming water.

"I got a green one!" Jacob exclaims and holds up a piece of washed glass before rinsing it and sticking it in his already bulging pocket.

"I got a white one!" Helen runs up to you smiling. She has no pockets in her pink sunsuit, so you store hers in one of yours, but first you hold it up to the sunlight like Jacob did.

"Look," you say, "it's got red in it."

Jacob and Lynn stop to look.

"That's a find," Lynn laughs.

"It's the best one so far," Jacob agrees.

Helen beams.

And you realize Helen and Jacob are not even fighting. And Jacob isn't saying anything about his being better and Helen isn't calling him *stupid* and everyone is so nice, it doesn't even feel like your real family.

"I want to go all the way to the end." Helen points to the cliffs.

"No. Let's stay here and get more treasure." Jacob begins to create a pile of glittering glass and wet shells.

Lynn looks at you. "What do you want, May?"

"I'll stay here with Jacob if you want."

Helen grabs Lynn's hand again, dragging her down the beach.

"Okay, come down and get us when you're done," Lynn calls over her shoulder.

"Look at this one, May." Jacob peels back your fingers and puts a piece of glass in your hand. "It has red in it like Helen's." You hold it up to the sun. It could be stained glass with red and golden brown streaks in it. Maybe it used to be a beer bottle. Jacob fishes for more, and you stand at the edge of the water and close your eyes, feeling the sun burn against your cheeks. It's like getting out of a hot bathtub on a winter day, only reversed. Your feet are numb and your face is on fire.

Next to Locker's Flower House and Promise Park, this is your favorite place in the world.

Jacob starts to sing a new song about water and wind and waves. About how everything makes a whoosh, whoosh, whoosh and all the sounds travel to the end of the Earth and never stop. Above his voice, you hear the waves roll into the beach, sometimes so loud that's all you can hear. It's like Jacob's chorus, like it's singing a lullaby with no words and you wonder what it would be like to sleep down by the water.

You think you would like it.

Jacob runs up beside you. "Can we go in the water?"

You look way down toward the end of the beach. Lynn and Helen are still walking. Helen's still got Lynn's hand, and Lynn's long blond hair is bouncing against her back.

"You're not wearing your swimsuit."

Jacob's T-shirt and his matching seersucker shorts are already soaked.

He peels off his T-shirt. "Now it's a swimsuit," he laughs and starts wading into the water, and the waves break against his body and push him back and he laughs and yells, "Come on May."

And you look one more time down at Lynn and Helen, and the beach is so long you can hardly see them, and you peel off your shirt, too, because even though it makes

Mother mad, you'd put your clothes over your swimsuit. You run into the water straight toward Jacob who splashes at you and shrieks with delight. The chill takes your breath away and the two of you splash and scream.

"Look, I'm a surfboard," Jacob flings his body against a whitecap.

And you laugh and play and splash in the water. Then you hear Lynn's voice, "May! Jacob!" and you turn to see her running back down the beach.

"Get out of the water!" She sounds mad.

Jacob's body rolls right into you and knocks you off your feet. He jumps up laughing and you scramble up and grab him and drag him with you back up to the sand.

"Come on, May, let's do it again. What's the matter, May?"

"No, no, no!" Lynn is handing you each your balled up T-shirts. "You must never, never, never swim alone."

"That's the first rule," Helen says. She runs up panting beside Lynn.

"That's right, that's the first rule."

Lynn's face is red.

"I was with him," you say.

"But you are not a lifeguard or an adult, May. Always make sure somene is watching when you go swimming."

"But I was watching him," you say again.

"*But* you are not an adult," Helen says.

"Shut up!" you tell her, and you feel your heart speed up and your hands ball up into fists and you want to pound her.

"We only went up to our waists." Jacob speaks in a muffled voice, through the white cotton T-shirt, which is now covered with sand.

Suddenly, your head feels like someone put it in a blender and everything starts spinning around, because you are certain that nothing bad happened, but Lynn is acting like it did. And now she is mad at you.

And it's your fault, but you were only doing what you were supposed to do, even though you played a little in the water. Jacob didn't get hurt. You would have never ever let anything bad happen to Jacob.

You were watching him just like she said.

You hate it when people get mad at you for no reason at all.

"I'm going to tell Mother," Helen threatens.

And suddenly it feels like someone shot an arrow straight through your heart. Because even though Mother is hundreds of miles away, everything bad that happens is your fault and you deserve to die and you crumple down and bury your head in your balled up T-shirt and start to cry, even though you never cry, and Lynn squats down beside you and says in a voice that isn't mad anymore, "It's okay, May. It's okay. You didn't know and now you do, so it's okay."

"Nothing bad happened," you cough out, looking up at her. She is all blurry. But she has blue eyes, even bluer than Dad's. And you want her to like you.

"That's right. Nothing bad happened. But even for lifeguards, the first rule is—never swim alone."

"No one got killed or drowned," you sob.

"Everything is going to be okay," she repeats softly.

You think *please don't hate me.*

She strokes your head.

"Oh no, it's happening again," Jacob points to the balled up shirt in your hands.

There's blood on it.

You taste the blood dripping off your upper lip.

"Oh jeese," Lynn says. She searches her back pockets and pulls out the light blue kerchief.

"May's nose always bleeds," Helen tries to reassure Lynn.

"Here, put your head back," Lynn says, and you want to say it works better not to put your head back, but you don't want to disobey her, so you lie back in the warm sand and she makes your T-shirt into a pillow and lays your head back on her knee and pinches the kerchief to your nose. And even though it doesn't hurt, you can't stop the tears streaming down your cheeks. They just keep coming and coming and coming. Helen and Jacob stand there staring down at you because they never see you cry. You want them to look away, so you close your eyes and rest your head on Lynn's knee and wait for the bleeding to stop.

It feels like hours pass. Then, you hear Lynn's voice.

"May?"

You open your eyes.

She is looking down at you. "I think it's stopped."

Helen and Jacob are both lying down in the sand beside you. Jacob is asleep and Helen props herself up on one elbow to examine your nose.

"It stopped," Helen agrees.

Gently, Lynn pulls her knee out from under your head and cradles it with her hands as she lowers it down to the sand. Then she gets up and rinses the bloody kerchief in the water. Jacob wakes up and looks at you.

"A wave must've knocked it."

"Yeah," Helen agrees.

Lynn leans over and touches the cool damp kerchief under your nose. Goose bumps jump out all over your body and you wrap your arms around yourself.

"The sun's going down," Lynn says. "It's getting cooler. We'd better get back and get you guys into dry things." She smiles and helps you pull the T-shirt back on over your head.

It's streaked with blood.

You follow her up the crooked sandy path back to the cottage.

The minute your foot hits the front step of the cottage, you see the smoke from the barbeque and hear Aunt Cleo's voice in the kitchen and already you feel better. Helen runs ahead and brings you a clean T-shirt before Grandmother sees the bloody one. Lynn throws the bloody one in the trash in the old outhouse just as your cousins come running onto the big front porch to greet you. Grandmother rings the dinner bell and makes everyone wash their hands and then she ushers all the kids into the giant dining room and when you see the table you just stare with your mouth wide open.

Like Helen and Jacob.

There are plates piled with steaming corn on the cob and china bowls with leafy green salads and cherry tomatoes, and buttered dinner rolls, and glistening reddish pork ribs covered in sauce, and tall sweaty glasses of lemonade and even though you can't smell any of it, you know it will taste a million times better than mashed potato flakes with lima beans.

Grandmother steps up behind you and directs everyone to their places. As soon as Jacob sits down, he starts to reach for a roll and Helen cries out, "Grandmother has to say grace."

"Rub a dub, dub, thanks for the grub," Jacob sings, but pulls back his arm to wait for Grandmother.

Everyone laughs, even you and Helen.

After Grandmother says the grace, you close your eyes and listen to everyone laugh and talk and pile food on their plates, and inside your heart feels happy because of the sounds. Especially Helen's laugh. This place is way better than Locker's Flower House or Promise Park, and you hardly even think about Mother and Dad.

You feel a bit bad about getting Lynn mad. Now you know—even though you've been taking care of people for forever, even though you're practically in high school, it doesn't matter— you're not a lifeguard, and you don't count as an adult. At least not according to Lynn.

It does help to know that even Lynn never swims alone.

CHAPTER 21

The Phone Call

THAT EVENING Aunt Cleo makes a fire in the fireplace and even though you offer to help, she insists on doing it herself. She wants to demonstrate how a really good fire is made. She used to be a Girl Scout leader and she knows how to make a fire with a bright blue flame, so that the smoke doesn't come back into the cottage. You watch her one arm deftly lift and rearrange a log that must weigh as much as Jacob.

Someday you want to be as strong as Aunt Cleo.

When the fire is good and crackling, she lets all the kids cuddle up in sleeping bags around her feet and she reads from *The Secret Garden*. You get to turn the pages, but she won't let you read because she says sometimes it's important to let yourself be read to. You want her to read and read and read, but Jacob falls asleep, and soon Grandmother announces that when Aunt Cleo finishes the chapter, it is time for bed.

It almost kills you when she stops at the part where Mary Lennox hears the noise of someone crying out in the night, and Martha is not fessing up. Martha, the housemaid, keeps saying it's only the wind. But you know she's lying, only you don't know why.

That night, you and Helen get to sleep out in one of the rooms that turns into a porch. Big screen windows surround the two twin beds, and the wind shuffles through the long thin needles of the white pines that brush up against the side of the cottage. The crickets and cicadas stop making noise just after Helen turns off the light, and then you hear the waves washing up on the beach below the cliffs, before the bugs start up again.

"These blankets smell funny," Helen complains in the dark.

You try to smell your blanket, but you can't. Your head is still floating around with Mary Lennox and Misselthwaite Manor with its hundred locked rooms and the hunchback uncle and most of all the strange cry from the corridor.

"May... does your blanket smell like mothballs?"

You don't answer. The truth is, even though you feel happy inside and you like to hear Helen laugh, you are still a little mad at her.

"May, I'm not really going to tell Mother you took off your shirt and went swimming."

You don't say anything. Without Marie around, Helen wants you to be your friend again.

Helen sighs.

You ignore her.

"I'm not sleepy," she says.

You lie there and listen to the sounds. You are not really sleepy either, but you don't really feel like talking until Helen asks, "Do you think the crying sound was really the wind?"

You prop yourself up on one elbow and look at her outline in the dark. "Nope."

"Do you think the hunchback's wife didn't really die, and he's keeping her a prisoner in one of the hundred locked rooms?"

"Nope."

"Then—who is crying May? You probably know and aren't telling me."

"I think…" you hesitate, "it's another kid."

"A kid?"

"Yep." You plop back down onto your back and close your eyes.

"A boy or a girl?" Helen asks.

This time you really don't know. You don't even have a hunch, so you pretend to fall asleep hoping Helen won't talk anymore.

It works.

A few minutes later you hear her whispering to herself, "It better not be a boy, I don't want a stupid pig boy like Jacob."

Is she talking about the book or the new baby?

Grandmother said we probably wouldn't hear about the new baby for a few more weeks, but the very next day, the phone rings and Grandmother calls you and Helen and Jacob back from the beach.

Lynn stays with all your cousins, but she yells from the water that you have to wear your new flip-flops and not go barefoot.

On the way back, Jacob starts to tease Helen.

"He's here. He's here. He's here."

"Who's here?" Helen asks.

"Our new brother."

"Stop being such a pig, Jacob. I hate you."

Before you can even tell Helen to stop, Grandmother calls from the front porch, "Is that any way to talk to your brother?"

"He keeps saying it's a boy and I want a sister," Helen whines.

Grandmother pays no heed, she herds you all into the kitchen where there is an old black dial phone on the wall. Aunt Cleo is holding the receiver. She hands it to Grandmother, and Grandmother says into the receiver, "Here they are," and she motions for everyone to put their ears in a circle around the receiver and out comes a sound so strange you and Helen and Jacob all wrinkle up your faces. Helen covers her ears.

"What is it?" You look up at Grandmother.

"I think… it's a donkey," Jacob suggests.

Helen temporarily takes her hands away from her ears to say to Jacob. "It is not a donkey, stupid!"

"That's enough." Grandmother shakes her head. You look up, because she sounds exactly like Dad.

Aunt Cleo has a mysterious grin on her face.

"What is it?" you ask again.

"Don't you know?" Grandmother laughs.

You look at Helen and shrug your shoulders.

Jacob starts to imitate it, "Heeehaaaw heeehaaaw heee-haaaw heee—"

"Don't!" Helen cries and covers her ears again. "Make him stop."

Grandmother and Aunt Cleo exchange a look. Grandmother puts her hand over the receiver and whispers, "It's your new baby brother."

Dad's voice comes out of the phone loud and clear, as if he is standing right there. "Did you hear that? May, Helen, Jacob? Did you hear that?"

"They heard it," Grandmother answers for all of you.

Then, she hands the phone to you, probably because you're the oldest.

"May?" Dad's voice sounds happy.

"Hi Dad," you answer.

"We named him Gabriel, but we're going to call him Gabe."

You turn and report this to Helen and Jacob.

"Gabe?" Helen repeats, like she has a mouth full of lima beans. "Isn't that a girl's name?" She asks hopefully.

Dad hears her. "Gabriel is a boy's name. Like the archangel."

A shadow crosses over Helen's face.

"He arrived early, but he's fine, just fine."

Jacob starts hopping up and down. "I want to hear him again. I want to hear the angel baby." Aunt Cleo places her stump on his shoulder to settle him down.

"Are you kids having a good time?" Dad asks.

You nod. No words come out of your mouth.

159

"I want to tell him. I want to tell him," Jacob grabs for the phone, but Grandmother is too fast, she pulls the receiver away and says, "I think they're all digesting the big news. Here's Jacob." She hands the phone over to Jacob, who immediately forgets about listening to the angel baby, "It's all sand and about a mile long… there are cliffs… and giant waves… and shells… and… tons of… washed glass… and me and Helen found one with red in it… and…."

The donkey sound breaks through again.

You look over at Helen. Her jaw is set tight, and she's just staring down at her feet. She's mad, but there are tears in her eyes, so she must be a little sad, too. You should have told her, so she'd have known and not been so disappointed. Then to your surprise, you see that Grandmother and Aunt Cleo, and even Jacob, all have tears in their eyes, too.

"I'd better get him back to your Mother," Dad's voice says, and there's a rustling sound on the other end of the line. "Your Mother sends her love. We'll call you kids again later, okay?" There is a click and the line goes dead.

Helen starts to cry. "I didn't even get to talk to him."

"My, my, this is big news, isn't it?" Grandmother hugs her and rubs her back, but Helen keeps crying. Even though she is thirteen now, she still cries a lot.

"Will Gabe come up and play with us at the cottage?" Jacob asks joyfully.

"No. But you'll get to go home and play with him in a few weeks," Aunt Cleo answers.

You touch at the edge of your own eye. No tears. You look around at everyone again. Helen feels sad, Jacob feels happy, but what do you feel? For some reason all you can think about is—

Hal.

It's been over two years now, and still, all you can think about is Hal.

"Let's go back down to the beach and tell the other kids," Aunt Cleo says.

"Yeah!" Jacob jumps up and down.

Grandmother keeps hugging Helen. "I think this one 's been staying up too late reading," she says and gets up and leads Helen by the hand back to her own bedroom where she will have Helen lie down and rest for a bit.

Following Aunt Cleo back to the beach, Jacob smiles at you. "See?" he whispers. "He came back."

You look at him, not sure what to say. He looks so happy, so relieved, really. He's wearing a Green Bay Packer football jersey with his name and the number 10. Aunt Cleo gave it to him on his last birthday. Part of you wonders why he still believes this when he is growing up as fast as you are, and another part of you wishes you could feel that certain about anything.

Probably this new baby is not Hal, but you can't help pondering. Will he have green eyes? You decide to wait and see. Just to keep Jacob happy you say, "Yep, we have a new brother."

Jacob whispers in a sing-song voice all the way to the beach, "*He came back.*"

Aunt Cleo waves to your cousins and Lynn who are playing in the mid-day sun. "It's a boy!" she hollers.

They cheer and run up forming a circle around you as waves wash gently onto the hot sand cooling your toes, which feel trapped in the flip-flops. Dozens of seagulls circle overhead and after Aunt Cleo shares the news, you decline the offer to go back out and you squat down at the edge of the water and spell *G-a-b-e* with your finger in the sand.

CHAPTER 22

The Angel

BACK INTO the water, Jacob runs singing out to your cousins and Lynn and the seagulls and the whole world. "He's here! He's here! He's here!"

You hear him shouting over the rush of the waves, "His name is Gabriel, like the angel, and we're going to call him Gabe."

You look down at the letters in the sand. A wave washes up and the G disappears. Aunt Cleo hangs back a short distance from the water and calls out, "Aren't you going in?"

You turn around and ask, "Can I walk to the end if I don't go swimming?"

For some reason you feel like being alone.

Aunt Cleo smiles, "Sure honey, just stay in sight. I'll wait here." And she sits down on a rock and dangles her bare feet in the water.

Your cousins and Jacob have lugged a styrofoam surf-board out onto the sand bar. They take turns trying to ride the waves but mostly fall off into the water, laughing.

Lynn calls, "Come play, May."

"Aunt Cleo said I could walk to the end." You point to the cliffs.

Lynn nods and then Jacob splashes her and she screams and turns to join the splashing frenzy.

You look back at Aunt Cleo. She raises her stump arm. Then, you turn and head down the beach. Your bare feet slap against the wet sand as you pick up your pace. Twice you turn around to make sure no one has followed, and when you feel far enough away from Aunt Cleo and Lynn and your cousins, when you are almost to the cliffs, you turn and face the water.

The water is wilder here.

It churns and churls and swirls around the cliffs.

About a hundred yards out is the place that Grandmother calls the breakwater, where people have piled big rocks to keep the waves from crashing so hard. There are moss and vines and little orange flowers growing right out of the rocks. There is a trickle of water dripping down the cliff into the sand, forming a shiny pool that looks clean, but you'd never drink it.

Lynn says it's as polluted as the other Great Lakes.

You lean down and pick up a piece of glass. It's shaped like a triangle. How did it get here? From a beer bottle, you think.

The wind is strong off the water. Little mists of spray feel like kisses on your cheeks. You're still wearing your swimsuit, but it's dry. You have a pair of jean shorts on over the bottom tank part but wish you'd worn a T-shirt too, because your shoulders feel like they are reddish and raw from the sun.

You toss the glass back into the foaming water and cover your eyes. The sun makes rainbows in the mist. The rainbows shift and shimmer and disappear and reappear with the waves.

Shimmering.

Undulating.

Red.

Orange.

Yellow.

Green.

Blue.

Purple.

And, you don't know why... but you start to think about God.

God. God. God.

You haven't thought about Him for while.

You've been trying to ignore Him.

God-Hal. Hal-God. God-Hal. It's like the two of them are lumped together, somehow. What will happen if God suddenly decides to take this new baby up to heaven, too?

You feel an iggle of worry. This new baby already has an angel's name and it still makes no sense to you, why didn't God take you up to heaven?

You are the oldest.

Hal hardly had a chance to live.

Ms. Leggly, who still checks in on you, even though she isn't your teacher anymore, says *pondering is not only permissible—it is good*. Now it doesn't matter if you ponder, because you can read, and you've graduated from Sacred Heart, so you'll be going to high school, no matter what. Ms. Leggly says some people need to ponder, and there are ways to keep your pondering private. She ponders all the time but people don't know it.

She says it's none of their business. Similar to not mentioning to Sister Francis what the kids call her behind her back. Even, if you agree.

Everyone, she says, has their own truth.

The mist leaves little rivulets of water on your face and waves crash against the rocks and the wetness feels cool on your feet.

Suddenly, you feel a strange pressure on your shoulder, like someone put a hand there.

"*May.*" You hear it clear as day.

You spin to see who is there, but no one is there, and your heart drums against your chest. "Who are you?" you shout, spinning around again.

But the voice doesn't answer and then, for some reason, you wonder if it is Hal, but you don't see his only-air body. So you yell, "Hal? Is that you?"

Then you start to feel a little afraid, because you think maybe it's not Hal, but God, and he is real, and he heard what you were thinking and now he's mad.

"I am not afraid of you!" you yell.

Then you feel it. Same as when the leprechauns came. The colors filling your heart.

You close your eyes and whisper, "Hal?"

You can feel him.

Standing.

Next to you.

Your heart explodes. Your brain begins to buzz. It feels as if the hum of a million radios are trying to tune into your head all at once. It feels like Hal and God are inside of you. Talking. Singing. It feels like Hal is God and God is Hal. They are the same and different at the same time.

It's like someone is speaking to you in a strange language that makes no sense, yet, you know what the words are saying, and you know, though you can't see him—Hal is standing next to you.

You think of Jacob, who can read music without ever being taught how.

It's like that. You know what you know.

It doesn't matter if anyone believes you.

You feel happy.

You look back and see Aunt Cleo still perched on a giant rock down at the end of the beach. She waves her stump arm and you race toward the water and kick at the waves and run all the way back down the beach until you collapse into her arms.

"Look at you, all soaked to the bone," she laughs, wrapping you in a beach towel.

You're getting tall, but not too tall for me to hug." She pulls you close. She smells like peppermint gum.

"So much for not getting in the water," she says. "You may as well have gone swimming." She wraps her stump arm around you and kisses the top of your head.

Your face is muffled in her shoulder. "Do you believe God talks to us?"

Aunt Cleo smiles. "I suppose... through his angels."

"What do they say?"

Aunt Cleo looks out across the water like she needs to think. "Well, I suppose whatever needs to be said."

"Have you ever heard one?"

Aunt Cleo laughs and nuzzles her chin against your head. "Oh, I hear them all the time." She cocks her head like she's listening to the wind. "Why, I think I hear one now."

You listen.

"Can you hear her?" Aunt Cleo asks.

You listen harder and shake your head. All the angels at Sacred Heart seem to be men. Mostly, you know about the archangels, Michael and Raphael, and you try to remember if Gabriel was an archangel, too, and you think that he was, and then there is Lucifer, who was definitely a man, until he got banished to Hell, until he turned into something more serpent-like, more demonic.

Aunt Cleo nods solemnly.

She closes her eyes like she's trying to concentrate. "Shhh, listen."

You want to ask her the names of the female angels so that you can tell Helen, but first you want to hear what Aunt Cleo can hear.

With your eyes closed you can feel the warmth of Aunt Cleo's arms around you and the rise and fall of her chest.

You think about telling her what happened, but instead, you listen. Aunt Cleo's breathing mixes with the wind and the waves and the sea gulls and Jacob's singing and the sound of your cousins splashing and playing in the water with Lynn.

After a minute or two, you open your eyes and whisper into Aunt Cleo's ear, "Is she still talking?"

"Shhh," Aunt Cleo says seriously. She keeps her eyes closed. "She just said something, but I couldn't quite make it out. I heard it, right here." She points with her stump arm to the ear you whispered into.

You laugh.

"Aunt Cleo!"

She opens her eyes and busts out laughing and hugs you so hard with her stump arm that you almost lose your breath.

CHAPTER 23

The Secret Garden

THE NEXT three months fly by.

The night before Dad is to arrive to take you and Helen and Jacob back home, Aunt Cleo finishes reading *The Secret Garden*. When the book ends you feel happy and sad at the same time. You wish Aunt Cleo could read to you every night for the rest of your life, and that books, like *The Secret Garden,* could go on and on.

Forever.

Aunt Cleo gives you the book to read again if you want.

That night, you tuck *The Secret Garden* under your pillow, and you and Helen push your beds up against the wall in the porch room because Grandmother has warned everyone there might be storms during the night. Jacob gets to sleep on a cot in Grandmother's room.

As soon as you crawl under the sheets a loud rumble and a clap of thunder shake the walls and rattle the windows. You look over at Helen. She's sitting on the edge of her bed holding her hands tightly over her ears and staring out the big window, the same window you helped Aunt Cleo close because her stump arm couldn't balance both sides of it.

You say to Helen, "Grandmother says it's the lake effect."

In the musky darkness, there's another bang, then the wind howls like a scream, like in *The Secret Garden,* and you hear wood splintering and the room explodes with light.

Helen squeezes her ears harder and whimpers.

The wind rattles the shutters. You jump out of bed and draw them up all the way to the top of the window, so they can't move around anymore.

Helen cries.

You go and sit on the edge of her bed.

"Tomorrow we go home," you say, trying to cheer her up, but it doesn't work. Rain begins to rat-a-tat-tat on the windowpanes.

"I think it'll stop soon," you say.

Helen turns and tries to push you off of the bed, then she slams her face down into the pillow and screams and cries in a muffled tantrum. Another rumble of thunder is approaching and you jump back in your own bed and cover your ears. When it hits, you feel electricity run through your body. Helen gets very quiet, then jumps up and runs shrieking out of the room. You follow her. In the dark hallway you run straight into Lynn.

"Where's she going?" Lynn is tying a white bathrobe around herself.

"I don't know," you say breathlessly, racing after Helen.

Lynn follows you down the steps. "Helen?"

Helen heads for Grandmother's room.

"No, Helen, don't wake them up, it's okay," Lynn calls, but Helen bangs through Grandmother's door. "Make it stop!" Helen shrieks.

Grandmother sits up and takes Helen into her long silky arms and coos, "Oh my, my, now, now, now, calm down."

Another bang, and Helen buries herself into Grandmother's arms.

Jacob, still half-asleep, turns toward the wall and murmurs something about needing more men on the front line.

"I tried to stop her," Lynn apologizes, but Grandmother waves her arm, "Oh, it's fine, you go ahead and go back to bed, they can stay with me until things settle down."

When Grandmother motions you toward her, you crawl up on the bed, too.

She edges closer to the wall. You and Grandmother form a sandwich around Helen, and Grandmother whispers, "Let her cry it out."

When she says this, it reminds you of Dad and you remember he is probably driving up to get you right now, because he likes driving during the night. You hope he will not get struck by lightning or caught in a flash flood or blown away in a tornado, and you hope he knows how bad the storms are with the lake effect and even though the cottage is the best place you have ever been, you feel Helen trembling beside you and another part of you just wants to be home, in your own bunk, with sounds you recognize.

It's easier that way, to figure out if bad things will happen.

CHAPTER 24

The Angel Baby

WHEN YOU wake up, Helen's hair is matted against your face and Grandmother is gone. You prop yourself up and look around. Jacob is still asleep, all curled around Grandmother's pillow. You lie back down, trying not to move, because you don't want to wake them. Dad's voice comes from the kitchen.

Your heart sighs because he is safe.

He's talking to Aunt Cleo.

About the tornados that ripped through the Midwest, and how he missed the bad spots.

"The tollway was a mess," he says.

"Well, it was fierce last night. It traumatized the kids," Aunt Cleo says, and the teapot whistle goes off.

"Especially Helen," Grandmother adds. "Poor dear came tearing into my room."

"Apparently," Aunt Cleo laughs, "Jacob and I were the only ones who slept through it."

Helen sits up beside you rubbing her eyes. "Is it done?"

"Yep," you say, "and Dad's here."

Helen shoves you aside and jumps down from Grandmother's bed and races for the door. Jacob practically leaps awake.

"Dad's here?" He says, sleepily, and leaps over you in a race with Helen.

You jump up and join them.

In the kitchen, Dad hugs all three of you and everybody talks at once. Above the din of voices, Jacob pellets Dad with questions, "Did you see the lightning? Did you hear the thunder? Did you have to stop the car? Is Mother coming with our new brother?"

"Whoa, whoa, whoa," Dad holds his hand up.

"I think they're a little excited," Aunt Cleo laughs.

"Your Mother misses you very much." Dad pats Jacob's head, "She's waiting at home with Gabriel."

"The angel baby?"

"Your new baby brother," Dad says.

Helen gets quiet. You hear her thinking. She wants to stay longer, she wishes her friend Marie could come up so she could bring her to the beach, but she doesn't want any more lightning.

Helen doesn't get her wish, because that afternoon Dad packs all of you in the Cadillac and you head for home. He says, "I have to get back to work. Money doesn't grow on trees, you know."

At first, you get to sit in the front with Dad because you are the oldest, then Jacob keeps singing and Helen is trying to read and she can't keep her ears plugged and read at the same time, so she starts to whine. Dad stops at a gas station and makes Helen sit in the front with him and you go back with Jacob, who eventually falls asleep with his head in your lap.

Then you fall asleep too.

When you wake up you are home, in your own top bunk. There is light streaming through the window and you hear the donkey sound coming from Jacob and Hal's room, but then you remember Hal is dead. His stuff is gone. It isn't his room anymore.

You listen for Mother and Dad but you don't hear anything.

Leaning down over the edge of the top bunk, you peer at Helen. Her face looks sad even in her sleep. The donkey sound suddenly stops and Mother murmurs something. Her voice sounds calm and nice, so you quietly crawl down the bunk ladder and go into the kitchen. The new shag carpet feels scratchy on your feet and the linoleum feels smooth and cold like wet sand on the beach.

Mother comes out of Jacob's room juggling the new baby in her arms. She is skinny again. She is smiling. She sits down in a kitchen chair and says, "I missed you," and you race toward her and she sets the baby down in a little bassinet on the kitchen table and hugs you with both arms.

"I missed you," she repeats. Inside, your heart does jumping jacks because it is so happy.

The baby starts to cry. Mother laughs. You both look at his wrinkled face, and above his noise, she says, "He wants to be held all the time." She laughs again, and picks him up and hugs him to her shoulder. He stops.

Jacob comes flying out of his room. "Mama!"

"This is your new brother," Mother says proudly, and she balances the baby and hugs Jacob at the same time. Then Helen comes into the kitchen and Mother puts the baby down again and hugs all of you together, and you feel Helen trying to push you and Jacob away, but you push back, and Mother says, "All right, all right," because the baby starts to howl.

Mother picks him up again and holds him in her arms. All three of you watch him wail.

Helen puts her hands over her ears. "Why is he crying?"

"He's hungry," Mother coos, and smiles at him. Calling him her little angel.

"Heeehawww heeehawww heeehawww—" Jacob falls to his knees and starts baying like a donkey.

"Make him stop!" Helen cries and points to Jacob. Gabe's sounds feel like fingernails scraping on a chalkboard.

You watch as a cloud crosses over Mother's face.

Panic presses against your belly.

Gabe's cries get louder and louder and then, in desperation, you hear yourself yell, "I get to feed him first! I'm the oldest."

Somehow, those words make the storm pass over Mother's face.

"I want you to all go get dressed now. May, help Jacob, because your father is coming home and he has something he wants to show you."

Helen rubs her eyes. She stares blankly at baby Gabe. "What?"

"It's a surprise," Mother says.

You hate surprises.

Helen grimaces.

"A surprise?" Jacob echoes.

Mother nods. "Now, go on… all of you," and she shoos you away and smiles and whispers something to baby Gabe and takes him into the living room to feed him herself.

Helen follows you and Jacob into his bedroom.

Everything looks different. There is a new white crib where Hal's crib used to be. It has blue and yellow blankets and it is filled with stuffed animals, but no Morgan dog. Above it there is a mobile, with little flying elephants.

Jacob brags. "My room got redecorated."

"It's for the baby, not you," Helen says sourly.

"He thinks Gabe is Hal," you whisper into Helen's ear.

She crinkles up her face.

"What did you tell her?" Jacob demands.

You don't want Helen to tell Jacob.

But she says, "Jacob, Gabe isn't Hal. Hal is buried. He's dead. D-e-a-d. Remember?"

Jacob's face falls. You put your arm around him and he shrugs you off and jumps onto his bed, saying to Helen, "You think you know everything, but you don't."

"Don't be so stuuuu—"

You reach over to block Helen's mouth. To stop her from saying it but she grabs your hand and chomps on it, hard, with her teeth.

"Oww, Helen… you idiot!" you yell, and you whack her head with the hand that is hurting. She starts to cry and grabs a handful of your hair, trying to yank it from your head but you grab her hand and squeeze it as hard as you can.

She hates you. Her eyes look scary and desperate, and suddenly, she looks at you and then smiles, a mean smile, and then, she bites down on her own hand. It starts to bleed.

Mother comes into the room, holding her angel baby, and you both let go.

Helen triumphantly holds up her bleeding fist.

"Look what May did!"

"She did it herself," you yell, but Mother doesn't believe you. She holds up the bleeding hand and hugs Helen.

"May, go to your room! Now!" She points to the door.

You know you are going to be sorry you were ever born. You look at Jacob and plead, "Tell her, you saw, Helen did it herself," but, on the bed, Jacob just starts to hum and rock like he can't hear you.

"I didn't wet the bed, I didn't," he says in a wobbly voice, as you leave the room.

You crawl up in your bunk to wait.

You are so mad at Helen, you don't know what to do, so finally, you lean over the edge of the bed and spit on her pillow. Hanging over the edge, you watch the wetness soak in and you wish you were dead, not Hal, and you say to him, like he is actually listening, "It's a good thing you're up in heaven."

After that, you must have gone into a time pocket. Because now, you're in the back seat of the Cadillac sitting between Helen and Jacob, and Dad and Mother are in the front seat, and Mother is holding baby Gabe, who is asleep, and Dad says, "Here we are."

He pulls the car up in front of a brick house in the middle of a field. Other big houses are scattered across the open fields. Everything looks new and clean and fancy, not anything like Pig Valley. Some homes still have construction trucks parked in front of them, and all the trees and shrubs and bushes look like babies.

Jacob presses his nose against the car window.

"Who lives here?" he asks.

Dad turns around from the front seat. "Well, soon we will."

"We will?" Helen repeats.

"We're moving?" you say.

Mother turns around and smiles, "What do you think?"

"Can we see inside?" Jacob asks.

"Sure," Dad says.

Everyone flings open car doors in excitement, but you crawl out stiffly, because though you don't remember Mother's punishment, your backside feels sore. You squint your eyes at Helen as she skips ahead.

Part of you wants to hate her.

She must sense what you are thinking because she turns and sings, "When we move here, I'm going to get my own room and a horse and Dad said we could have a swimming pool and Marie can visit me every day."

Dad looks at Helen and laughs. "I hate to disappoint you honey, but the horse and the swimming pool will have to wait."

Helen giggles.

With his free hand Dad holds the door for you, Jacob, Mother, and Gabe.

As you step onto the shiny slate floor of your soon-to-be new home, Dad doesn't see Helen sticking her tongue out.

You close your eyes and stand there just inside the door listening to Mother introduce her angel baby to your new home.

CHAPTER 25

The Headaches

IN THE months that follow, you start school at Sacred Heart High, which is right next to the grade school. The two schools share the same building, so you still see Helen and Jacob at mass every morning. It doesn't feel very different, except now, you have different teachers for different subjects.

Mother and Dad are busy getting ready for the move to the suburbs. Baby Gabe grows bigger and louder, and although someone always picks him up when he cries, he cries a lot.

Mother calls him her Fussy Boy.

Luckily, she doesn't get as mad, like she did with Hal, and so far, she has not hit him. It is clear to everyone, even when he pushes away from her, he's her favorite. She calls him touch-defensive. Which means he can't stand to be held too much, so she must force him to sit in her lap and get hugs to get used to being touched. Maybe, eventually, he will like it.

She says, "It's for his own good."

She encourages you and Helen and Jacob to hold him, but he never sits still long enough, unless he's almost asleep.

You can't wait to move to the country and go to a public school. You're starting to hate Sacred Heart. Especially math. Math with letters makes no sense. You and Yvonne are in the same algebra class and the teacher reminds you of Sister Francis.

Yvonne calls her *The Nun Without the Penguin Suit*.

Every day, usually during math, your head starts to hurt. Sometimes so bad you can't concentrate and then you get sent to the nurse's office and she sends you home early to sit with a hot pad on your head. The nurse suggests Mother take you to the special doctor for x-rays, but the doctor says there is nothing wrong with your head, so Mother thinks it's just a ploy to come home early.

You don't tell them that whenever your head hurts, it is usually because you're trying not to think about Hal. But the more you try not to, the more you think....

Hal. Hal. Hal.

Whenever you hold Gabe you think about....

Hal. Hal. Hal.

And when Gabe cries, which he always does, the sound scrapes against your brain and you remember how Hal's cries used to make Mother mad. At least with Gabe, Mother doesn't go berserk.

Most days, except when you come home early, she seems almost happy.

CHAPTER 26

The Suburbs

There are unexpected delays with the new house. Dad says we'll move at the end of the school year, but then there are more delays, and by the time you actually do move, school is starting again.

Now you and Helen must take a yellow school bus to the public high school. Jacob takes a different bus to the middle school. Five days a week the two buses come to the same corner to pick you up and drop you off.

It is way too far to walk. Anywhere.

The sprawling stone house sits on top of a hill with no trees.

All you can see for miles is more big lots with brown trimmed houses like yours.

No sidewalks.

No brewery whistle.

No forklifts.

No idling semis.

No cabs or city buses.

No traffic to speak of.

Not even any sidewalks. And most of all . . .

No sounds. Just silence. And you notice it even more because there are . . .

No smells.

None.

No yeast.

No barley.

No Ambrosia Chocolate.

No hides drying in the wind at the tannery.

No monkey chow or dog chow or any kind of chow you can imagine.

No smell of anything to remind you if you are...

dead or alive.

CHAPTER 27

The Sign

INVISIBLE, THAT'S how Helen says she feels here.

This is because your family moved from Pig Valley, and she says most of the people who live in Pig Valley are poor, and this isn't really the country anyway, even though Dad keeps calling it that. It's really the suburbs, and people in the suburbs are snotty, so Marie's Dad won't let her come visit because we live on a street with millionaires, and he doesn't want Marie getting any fancy ideas.

You feel sad for Helen that Marie can't visit, but you point out that at least she didn't have to stay at Sacred Heart for ninth grade and have *The Nun Without the Penguin Suit.* But you know how she feels because you miss Yvonne, too.

You don't fit in either.

The other girls all go over to each other's houses after school, but the rule for you and Helen is to come straight home to help Mother. This is especially important now that Helen has noticed Mother is getting fat again.

187

"I don't want another baby in this stupid family," she says that night. You are lying side by side on the new twin beds in the bedroom you share at the end of the long hallway. Your door is cracked so you can hear Gabe if he happens to wake. Now it is your job to take care of Jacob and Gabe in the nighttime. Jacob does not have to keep his door open because when it is quiet he doesn't have nightmares. It was the nightmares that used to make him wet his bed. They've stopped in the new house. Your bedrooms are a mile away from Mother and Dad's. Theirs is huge, with a vaulted ceiling, on the other side of the giant rambling ranch house.

"She already has her stupid angel baby," Helen sighs.

"Maybe it will be a girl," you whisper in the dark.

"Who cares?" Helen says too loud.

"Shush, you'll wake Gabe."

"I don't care." Helen turns away and pulls the covers over her head. You listen for Gabe's cries, but he is quiet.

"I hate this family," Helen says into her pillow and then she starts to cry and all you do is listen until she falls sleep.

Another baby.

How do you feel about it?

The next day after school, Mother has you and Helen help with Gabe's toilet training. At first, it is fun, like playing dolls with a real doll, something you never got to do with Hal. It takes two because Gabe keeps trying to wiggle away and grab your hair and whap at your faces with his little fist. The only way to get him to sit still is to read him books.

He talks all the time now, but his favorite word is "Ha." So every time he tries to grab your hair he says, "Ha."

"Helen, take Gabe for a walk. May, I want you to come in here and help me." Mother's voice echoes down the hall from the kitchen.

You look at Helen, who is still wrestling with Gabe. So you grab his other hand and both of you swing him between you down the hallway like it's a game.

Gabe squeals with joy.

"Mmmm, what smells so good?" you ask, swinging Gabe into the kitchen.

"Chicken and dumplings," Mother says, as she warns happily, "Be careful not to pull his poor little arms out of their sockets."

While Helen gets Gabe outside you stand in the kitchen. Jacob is downstairs singing a song he heard on the radio. You recognize it. The Jackson Five. If Dad hears him singing that kind of music, he will make fun of Jacob. He will say that Jacob's hair isn't kinky enough for Motown. But you always tell Jacob to keep singing, and not to listen to Dad, because Dad is not always right about things.

You take in the sweet, starchy, spicy smells, and they make you feel so good, you double-fold all the napkins and wash all the pots and pans and get out the good green glasses and set the table. Mother lets you stir the gravy and it bubbles up around the dumplings and looks exactly like the lava that came out of Jacob's plaster volcano for his fifth grade science project. Mother laughs when you tell her this and she hugs you and you feel glad that it was Helen's turn to take Gabe for a walk.

At dinner, since the cat is out of the bag about another baby, Dad lets everyone pick names.

She doesn't care if it's a boy or a girl, Helen claims, but she only picks girls' names. "Sarah or Hannah or Rose."

"Jamie or Jeremy or James," Jacob says, "Something that starts with a J."

"What about you, May? Do you have any baby names you like?"

You are too busy eating to answer. Your mouth is too full of chicken to say, like Helen, you hope the new baby is a girl. Dad laughs when you finally swallow and ask, "Can I have another chicken leg while I think about it?"

That night Dad comes to your side of the house to say good-bye. He's going to a special business meeting because he is going to start his own company. He's wearing a new brown suit and matching shiny shoes and he sits down on the end of Helen's bed and says, "Your Mother tells me you girls have really been a help—"

Helen interrupts him, "Why do we have to have another baby?"

Dad pauses. "I'm counting on both of you to keep pitching in."

"You don't know what she's like," Helen says to Dad.

"Sometimes she's nice," you tell Helen because it's true and you don't want Dad to think you haven't been doing your job.

Helen flops back in her bed and covers her face with her sheet. "Dr. Jekyll and Mrs. Hyde," she whispers.

"That's enough, Helen. Your Mother works her fingers to the bone and you need to start respecting her."

"*We* do all the work," Helen retorts.

In the dusky light, Dad puts his hand up. "That's enough, Helen." He stands up and looks down at you.

"We all have to do our part. I've got enough on my plate just keeping all of you fed. You both know how your Mother is. Just do what she asks and everything will work out."

He rubs his big hands together and turns and leaves the room.

You listen to his feet thumping down the long hallway.

For some reason you are kind of excited about a new baby, but you hope it won't fuss as much as Gabe.

Helen comes back out from under her sheets. "I hate you," she whispers, but she doesn't cry.

What's this new thing you hear in her voice?

Jacob's shadow appears in the doorway. "May, I can't sleep, will you tell me a story?"

"God, Jacob, why do you act like such a baby? You're in fifth grade, aren't you over the story thing, yet?" Helen pulls a Glamour magazine out from under her pillow and slaps it down.

"A scary one?" you ask, because Jacob has gone from hating scary stories to wanting you to tell him one practically every night.

He nods and turns to Helen. "I'm telling Mother you took her magazine."

"Go ahead. Go tell her right now. I dare you." Helen flips a few pages.

Jacob stands in the doorway. He scowls at Helen and then turns back to you. "Please, May?"

"Go into his room," Helen says snottily, "I don't want to hear you guys." She grabs the flashlight off of the bedside table, pulls an Archie comic book out from under her pillow, stacks it on top of the magazine, flips the sheets back over her head and starts to read.

Aunt Cleo sent the comics in the mail. Helen loves them almost as much as fashion magazines.

She sent more postcards, too. One with a picture of people swimming with the dolphins, it made you so happy that you taped it on the ceiling above your bed so when you wake up every morning you can see the dolphins smiling down at you. Someday Aunt Cleo is going to take you swimming with the dolphins just like the people in the picture. Sometimes you can even feel the water against your face when you think of it.

You follow Jacob into his room.

"Tell me story," Helen mimics.

"Shut—" You cover Jacob's mouth.

"Shhhhh—"

Though you agree with Helen that Jacob is probably getting too big for stories, you are oldest, and you'd much rather stay up 'til midnight telling Jacob stories than run the risk that Mother will hear noises and come down to your side of the house.

Jacob has Grandpa JJ's old double bed. It feels huge compared to yours, so you crawl in beside him where the two of you lie side by side in the dark. He smells of stale socks and old milk, much better than the old days of diaper pails and pee sheets.

"Not the one about the hand that comes out of the box," Jacob says.

Tonight, you can only remember the one about the hand that comes out of the box and thump thump thumps its way up the stairs. So you ask him to tell you one instead.

But he whispers, "I want the new baby to be a boy, because then Hal'll get a second chance."

"What about Gabe?"

"He isn't him."

"I thought you said he was."

Jacob shifts in the dark. His voice sounds disappointed.

"No, he's not him. I know who he is. He used to be a general in my army, but I shrunk down and came back first."

This makes perfect sense to Jacob, so you don't say anything. You simply lie there feeling the warmth of his body next to yours. You wish you had your own room, like Jacob, so you wouldn't have to deal with Helen. You doubt you'd get lonely.

"A general is like being the boss," Jacob explains. "And since I came back first, I get to boss him."

Secretly, you agree that Gabe is not Hal.

Not just because Gabe has blue eyes and hair so blond it's almost white, but because of how Gabe is. When Hal looked at you, it was like his eyes could talk. Sometimes, he sat so still he didn't seem like a real baby at all.

Gabe never stops moving.

Or crying.

Like he has a supercharged battery pack in his brain.

Jacob falls asleep beside you. Like you do every night, you wonder if Hal can see you or if he's even looking, or if God makes him do chores and help the archangels with their duties.

The Archangel Michael is the one who is supposed to protect children. At Sacred Heart there's a painting of him in the hallway near the gymnasium. He's dressed like a Roman soldier. In his hands there's a sword with blood on it from slaying the serpent. He has green eyes and brown hair just like Hal and you and your Mother.

Jacob starts to snore softly. You snuggle in closer.

And try to stop thinking about Hal.

Why didn't the Archangel Michael protect Hal? Where was he on the day of the accident? Why didn't he come and tell you not to take Helen and Jacob to your cousins'?

The next thing you know Dad is in Jacob's room shaking your shoulder.

"May? May?" he whispers. "Wake up, honey."

You open your eyes.

His finger is to his lips. "Shush, don't wake your brother." Urgently, he motions you to follow him into the kitchen.

It is still pitch black outside.

"What time is it?" you whisper as your foot lands on a dark wet spot in front of the stove. You look down to see what spilled on the kitchen carpet. There isn't an empty pot, pan, or pitcher in site.

Dad looks at his watch. "Three… now listen, May, your Mother's water broke early, I've got to take her to the hospital." His voice sounds panicked. "Make sure Helen and Jacob get off to school and take care of Gabe 'til I get back, okay?"

You step off the wet spot.

"When are you coming back?"

Dad shakes his head. He looks scared. Like he did the day Hal died. Your stomach starts to feel like an elevator going down way too fast.

Mother moans from the garage. Dad rushes to the door. "I don't know, but you're in charge. You take care of the others, okay?"

You nod.

His Titus Tannery workshirt is on backwards and he's wearing loafers without any socks. He hardly wears his old clothes anymore and it's funny to see him dressed like this.

"I'm counting on you, May," he says as he runs out.

After the Cadillac peels off out of the driveway, you rub your eyes and lean down on your haunches. The wet spot is about two feet wide and three feet long. How much water came out? Why didn't the baby come too?

How early is it? One month? Two?

You never asked.

A part of you was trying not to think about another baby.

You lean down and sniff the wet spot.

It smells like the river in Promise Park. Suddenly, you remember the blind man on the bridge, how you were late getting home, how you thought you'd get in big trouble, but then no one noticed because they were all distracted by the shiny new floor.

This spot is way bigger than the blood spot.

"Is it a boy or a girl?" you say out loud, as if Hal or God or the Archangel Michael will answer. "I can't tell this time...."

Nothing happens.

"Please tell me." You whisper softly because a part of you is afraid and a strange tightness begins to choke in your throat. It's not a getting sick kind of tightness, more like an invisible rope someone is tying tighter and tighter around your neck. For the first time since Hal's funeral, you sink to your knees and bow your head. "Please don't take this baby, too. If you need another angel, please, please, take me."

Your ears start to buzz.

You stay still and listen hard.

Nothing happens.

Something is wrong. You don't know what, you just know that something is wrong. You think about waking Helen to show her the spot, but decide not to because the buzzing stops and if it is a bad sign you don't want her to cry.

Instead you go and get a bunch of kitchen towels and lay them down over the spot and press down with your feet. Then you put the soaked towels on the top step because you're too afraid to go down into the basement.

Helen calls you a chicken.

She makes a "braaaack, braaack, braaack" sound and flaps her arms at you for being afraid of the basement in this new house, but it is twice the size of the one in Pig Valley, and Jacob saw a ghost soldier in the back work-room and although you know how Jacob is, you decide to wait until morning. You go back to bed to wait for Helen and your brothers to wake up.

"May? Helen?" Dad is standing between your two beds shaking both of you on the shoulder at the same time.

You and Helen sit up in unison.

The bedroom is flooded with light.

Jacob comes running in and flops down on the end of your bed.

"You have a new brother," Dad announces, "He came out breech and a bit blue, but he's okay."

Dad's face is red and blotchy but he's smiling.

"What's breech?"

"Feet first," he says, tousling your hair. "The umbilical cord got wrapped around his neck and cut off his air, so the doctor had to work fast."

Your ears begin to buzz louder than before. You remember the invisible rope around your throat. Did God hear your prayer? Was Hal with him? Was the Archangel Michael paying attention this time? Now, it doesn't matter if this new baby is a boy or a girl, you're just glad God let him live.

"What's his name?" Jacob asks.

Helen looks at you. She's disappointed. Later you will tell her about the spot and the invisible rope and she will be glad because she doesn't want any more babies to die in your family, either.

"James," Dad says to Jacob. "His name is James."

His eyes are still watery but not scared anymore.

"Yes!" Jacob jumps up and claps his hands. "His name starts with J."

He starts to play an air guitar and rhyme all sorts of "J" words.

"Jacob and James went jumpin' with the Jivin' Java Cats, just in time for the jelly-belly—"

Helen covers her ears.

Dad laughs.

You laugh, too. Not because of Jacob, but because now you know the buzzing was a sign, a sign that everything would be okay, and you think you are starting to understand Spirit talk, even if you don't know who is talking it. It is nothing like real talk, because you can feel it come in through your heart, and it starts to happen again while you are sitting there on your bed, you feel it, in your heart, and you whisper, "Thank you."

In case God or Hal or the Archangel Michael or any other angels are still listening.

CHAPTER 28

The Bottle Lesson

WHEN DAD brings Mother and baby James back home from the hospital, Gabe goes crazy, running around in circles until he's so dizzy he throws up the oatmeal you fed him for breakfast. Then Helen cries because Dad makes her clean it up instead of you, and he lets you sit on the sofa and hold the new baby because you are the oldest.

Mother takes Gabe by the hand and goes straight to bed. She leaves baby James with all of you.

"You kids keep the noise down. Your Mother needs to rest," Dad says as he watches Mother and Gabe go down the hall. As soon as her door clicks shut he explains why Mother and baby James had to stay longer at the hospital. Because James came out backwards they had to do a special operation on Mother.

"Did he take out her appendix?" Jacob asks

Dad shakes his head.

"No, the doctor tied her tubes. It's too dangerous for her to have any more babies."

"Not—ever?" Jacob asks.

Dad shakes his head.

Helen looks at you. She's started wearing makeup and there's mascara smeared on her cheek.

She sighs.

Next to you, Jacob squints his eyes at baby James. "Can I hold him?" he asks.

"Me next." Helen wipes her eyes.

Dad takes baby James and hands him to Jacob.

"Wipe your face first," he tells Helen, and she races to the bathroom for a tissue.

Dad doesn't like Helen wearing mascara. But practically all the girls in the public high school wear it. Helen let you try hers, but it made your eyes itch.

Jacob studies baby James. He is fast asleep and it is impossible to see his eyes, but he has blond hair like Gabe's, though he is much much fatter.

"He's heavy." Jacob tries to swing him up and down but Dad makes him stop.

Then Helen returns and Dad whisks James out of Jacob's arms into Helen's. "Your sister's turn." Helen settles in on the other side of you.

Baby James suddenly wrinkles his face and wiggles in her arms.

"He's waking up." There is wonder in Helen's voice.

You all watch as baby James opens his eyes and looks around.

They say that babies can't see much after they are first born, only shadows, but baby James seems to be looking at everyone, then he focuses in on Helen, who smiles at him and says shyly, "Hi." And baby James actually smiles back.

"He must know you," Jacob whispers.

You all stare at his joyful jowly face.

"He's so happy," you whisper.

"He's glad to be home," Dad says. He reaches to take James back but Helen is so mesmerized she tightens her hold on the baby blanket.

"He's going to be hungry pretty soon," Dad warns.

The minute he says this James opens his mouth and howls. Helen's eyes get big like an owl. "Okay, okay, take him," she cries, and Dad does.

Helen covers her ears.

Dad laughs.

You and Jacob laugh, too.

"Feed him. Feed him," Helen begs.

Dad cradles baby James in one arm and pulling a bottle out of his top shirt pocket, he sticks it in James' mouth. Instantly, the noisy cries become the sound of hungry sucking.

"That a boy," Dad laughs.

Helen drops her hands and starts to giggle.

James reaches for the bottle. "Can I hold it?"

You don't think this is a good idea. "You have to hold his neck up. Me and Helen should learn to feed him first so we can help Mother."

Dad agrees. He hands baby James back to you. "You show 'em how, May. This is gonna be your job now. Your

Mother's got to rest, so you give 'em bottle lessons." He goes off to shower for work. You and Helen and Jacob spend the rest of the day cuddling baby James and feeding him an endless supply of bottles, which he seems to want to suck on whenever he is awake.

You discover as long as he is being fed he doesn't cry.

In the days that follow James grows larger and larger. You teach Helen and Jacob how to boil his bottles and clean the plastic nipples and test the temperature and burp baby James.

The days slip into months and the months into summer and the summer, once again, slips into fall. By the time school rolls around James is almost two years old and he weighs close to thirty pounds, and Helen and Jacob really don't want to feed him much anymore, so most of the time you prop him up with his bottle in a swing that winds up and you let him suck and suck and suck until he falls asleep.

CHAPTER 29

The Wine

IN THE suburbs there are no Catholic schools and every-body goes to the same high school, so now you take a different bus than Helen, who catches the freshman bus, and Jacob, who is in junior high. You are the last one to get picked up.

Every morning when it's time to catch the bus, you can hear Helen and Jacob arguing all the way to the corner.

If this were Pig Valley their voices would be drowned out by traffic noises and idling trucks, but out in the suburbs, there are too many empty spaces and their voices bounce back over the rolling green lawns into the sprawling stone house.

"Oh for God's sake," Mother says, coming into the kitchen. Dad is still getting dressed.

"Should I put Gabe in his car seat?" you ask. You've stayed back to help.

"You'd better wait. Your father's still poking around in there."

You make Gabe sit on the kitchen floor and hand him his two favorite toy trucks and go get ready for school. As you pull on a new stiff pair of blue jeans, you hear Mother shouting at Dad.

She is mad that he is still never home to help out. She says she's goddamnsickandtired of him running off to his playpen everyday while she is left with all these kids, but you don't hear Dad say anything. Then you hear the garage door open and the car drive off.

James is asleep on Helen's bed.

She got up and fed him his bottle earlier this morning because you put the boys to bed last night, and that was the deal the two of you made.

Every night before you go to bed, you and Helen have to negotiate who will do what because after her operation, Mother almost never comes down to your side of the house to help. Dad is hardly ever home, and if he is, he just sits in the family room and drinks martinis and smokes and reads the paper, so you and Helen must do it. And you don't know why, but suddenly, you hate getting up early and most days you really just want to stay in bed and skip school, though you don't. You go even if you're sick, because Mother hates it if anyone stays home from school.

When Jacob had his appendix out, she made him stay in his room all week to rest. He wasn't allowed to come out to the kitchen to get a glass of water until she got up from saying her rosary and taking a nap.

In the suburbs you seem to get sick a lot, not with headaches but with a stuffy nose, and Helen hates it when you snore, but you can't help it. The last time Aunt Cleo came to visit she said you both have allergies and there is no cure so you'll just have to learn to live with it.

Finished dressing for school, you carefully tuck the blankets up around James' solid little shoulders. He's clutching Helen's nightgown in his pudgy hands.

James almost never cries anymore.

You take his empty bottle and lean down and kiss his warm, sweaty forehead, closing the door quietly behind you.

All you and Helen really need to do is feed him or, when he is not eating, plop him in the wind-up swing chair and crank the handle, and it never fails to rock him to sleep.

Helen calls it, "The babysitter's babysitter."

In the kitchen, Mother is sitting at the kitchen table with a sweating bottle of Pepsi in front of her. She's wearing the white bathrobe she got when she went to the hospital.

"Should I put James in his chair?" you ask.

She says nothing.

She just stares out the west window into the acre lot behind your new house where they are building another house, even bigger than yours.

"Should I…?" you stop and look at Mother. It's like she doesn't even know you are there. If you waved your hands in front of her face would she even blink? You place the empty baby bottle in the sink.

The sink is piled with dirty breakfast dishes. Jacob was supposed to empty the dishwasher, now you or most likely Helen, because she gets home first, will get stuck with them after school.

Jacob has piano lessons. The band director thinks he's some kind of protégé because he can read music without even learning how.

Mother takes a long puff on her cigarette.

"He's asleep on Helen's bed," you say.

Mother doesn't acknowledge you as you walk out the door.

When you get home from school that day things are almost exactly as you left them, except that Mother has gone back to her room to take a nap. The empty Pepsi bottle is still on the table. The huge pile of dishes is still in the sink, and Helen is lying beneath James' wind-up swing reading one of the Archie comics that Aunt Cleo sent, while James' eyelids float up and down, the motion of the swing lulling him to sleep.

"Where's Gabe?" you ask.

"With Mother, where else," Helen mumbles without looking up.

"Is Jacob home yet?"

Helen shakes her head, still reading, and adds, "I'm not doing his dishes, either."

Just looking at all the dishes in the kitchen makes you tired. The house smells like a stale ashtray and your nose starts to plug up. You listen in the direction of Mother's room, but hear nothing, so you decide to do the dishes but to be quiet about it.

You turn the warm water on low.

It feels so good that you just let the water run and run and run.

You think about the dolphin postcard that Aunt Cleo sent and you wonder what it would be like to swim with dolphins. If they can really talk to you, like they do sometimes when they come to you in your dreams.

Helen appears in the doorway.

"Dad's got a meeting tonight."

You shut the water off and sigh. You and Helen will be in charge of dinner.

"We had grilled cheese last night," you say, irritated.

Helen shrugs.

"It's better than hot dogs."

Hot dogs are about the only thing you like that you can cook. You don't say anything.

"May?" Mother's voice calls from behind her closed door.

You and Helen look at one another. Shrugging again, Helen turns and goes back to the living room.

"I'm coming."

You take your time about it.

Mother's bedroom door is locked and you hear her tell Gabe to open it.

Gabe's fast feet patter across the giant bedroom and the handle turns and the lock clicks open. "Ha! I let her in. I let her in." Gabe says, as he races back to the king size bed, leaps up beside her, and picks up his Cat in the Hat book.

"I'm reading to Mother," he laughs.

"Yes," Mother smiles at him, "and... yurrr doing... a good job."

Mother is propped up against all the pillows on the bed. She's still in her nightgown, but she's wearing a silk bed jacket over her shoulders. It came in the same box as Aunt

Cleo's Archie comics and the dolphin postcard. Her left hand is wrapped in a peach-colored towel and her right hand is holding a pearly pink rosary.

She sets the rosary down on the side of the bed next to an empty wine glass.

Above the bedside table a picture of the Mother Mary holding Baby Jesus hangs lopsided on the wall.

She motions you to come sit by her.

You do.

"May honey, help me strip this wax off."

She begins to unfold the towel with her free hand.

You and she begin to peel the pliable wax off her fingers. When she dipped her hand in the big wax tank, probably about a half hour ago, it was a hot clear liquid. Now the wax feels like lukewarm plastic. Together you pile the waxy pieces up in the towel and you carry them back to the linen closet where she keeps the wax tank. Carefully opening the cover you scrape them back inside. Waves of heat rise toward your face. You watch the wax melt back into the clear liquid.

"Ha! Thing one and Thing two…." Gabe pretends to read to himself.

"I want you and Helen to get dinner tonight," Mother says behind you.

"Ha! Didn't know what to do…."

Putting the cover back you notice a spot, a dark spot, near your foot. You lean down to touch it, to make sure you didn't spill wax on the floor. The carpet is wet. You wipe at it with your fingers until the dampness rubs off onto your fingers holding your hand up in the dim light.

It's cherry red.

You put your finger to your lip, it's not wax, it's not blood, it tastes sour. Suddenly, your head begins to buzz louder than ever before and it feels like a time pocket, except everything around you starts to spin, and you grab the shelf because it feels like you are going to fall backward, but instead, you fall forward, and bang your head on the closet shelves as your body thump, thump, thumps to the ground. Then everything goes black. Before you can open your eyes again, you hear Gabe echoing Mother's words, "Ha! She fainted."

Now Helen is crouched beside you holding a glass to your lips. Mother is standing in the doorway of the linen closet saying, "Tilt her head, slowly."

Helen does.

The cool, clean glass feels good on your lips.

You take a long sip of water and open your eyes.

"May, what in the world? Did you get a shock?" Mother steps around your feet and unplugs the tank like it is a rabid cat, and then she cautiously shoves it back on the shelf. "I got one earlier. I told your father it wasn't safe in there, but he insisted it was fine. Oh, honey… " Mother kneels down next to you and Helen, "… are you okay?"

You look up.

"Oh, I'm so so sorry." Mother touches your forehead. You blink your eyes and try to remember what happened. Your head feels like someone filled it with dryer lint. Mother strokes your forehead. Her fingers feels warm from the wax, it feels so good you don't want her to stop, and you close your eyes because you don't care anymore, you don't care what made this happen, all you know is that this is the first time you have ever really felt that Mother cares about what happens to you.

"Ha! She got a shock."

Mother hugs Gabe and looks down at you with worried eyes. Then, for just a moment, a single second, really, you see your Mother, really see her: she looks like a scared little girl. You try to keep your eyes open and look at her, but they close by themselves and it feels like you are going into a time pocket, except it's different than it ever was before and you see yourself standing in a park next to Mother, who is even younger than you are now. She looks at you. Her eyes are green and clear, her hair is longer than yours, tied in ponytail braids on the side of her head, and she has freckles, just like you. She's jumping rope and singing a happy song, but then a man's voice comes from behind a tree and he calls her name and she stops and looks around like she wants to run. You whisper, "Who is he?" but it's like she can't see you.

Now the buzzing begins to turn into sounds and then words and then voices, only it's different than a time pocket because it feels like it is happening right now, and because it feels like your mother can hear you, and she needs your help. Somehow, you sense she's forgotten something, something bad that happened, something she needs to remember, but she can't, so you to need to remember—for her.

She starts jumping rope again, faster and faster, until sweat beads on her forehead and the rope cuts into her hands and blood drips on the grass and the man starts rubbing himself up against the tree and caressing his hands up and down the bark calling her name and motioning for her to follow and you feel frightened for her and you whisper, "Don't go," and she looks around like she can hear you and says, "His name is Oliver, he's not really my uncle but no one believes me," and she takes his hand and follows him into the woods—

"NO! DON'T!" you call after her.

She doesn't look back.

A part of you, like Jacob would say, the part of you that has lived a million lifetimes, understands she has no choice, she has to follow him, even though he really isn't her uncle.

"MAY? What's the matter? It's okay. Open your eyes, honey."

Your body convulses, your mouth is filled with blood, you sit up, choking, and coughing into the towel Helen holds near your face. Mother coos, "It's okay. It's okay." She grabs a washcloth off the shelf and hands it to Helen, "Get it wet," she says, and Helen runs off and Gabe just stares, and suddenly you remember and try to look down at the spot, but Mother has your head in her lap.

"May, don't move."

"The flllllooor," you try to say, "blood on the flllllooor."

"We need to get the bleeding stopped first."

And you let your head rest back in her lap and she strokes your forehead, and your eyes begin to close again but you force them back open because now you see rows and rows of red wine bottles on the bottom shelf—hidden behind stacks of clean towels. And you realize what you tasted.

Wine. Sour red wine.

CHAPTER 30

The Battle

BY THE time you turn sixteen, you have grown accustomed to the suburbs. Gone are the busy streets with black boys tossing coins on the sidewalk in the sweltering summer sun, gone is the mulatto blind man with his mute dog, gone the sounds of idling semis and buses and taxis and police sirens on Point Road. Now, what you hear is mostly silence.

Even with the windows open, it is usually quiet outside.

People who live in the suburbs do not talk about their families or problems or secrets. They talk about country clubs and cars and which stock option has great potential. For you there is not time to talk about anything, because the babies keep coming, and you are oldest, and you must help Mother because Dad depends on you.

This is just the way it is.

Until high school you have never liked school much, and what you like about high school is not being home.

Two months into your junior year, the gym teacher asks if you'll try out for the girls' basketball team.

"Come to the gym after school," Coach Crowe suggests.

She knows you usually have to go home and help after school. That's why you've never tried out before, but she's been watching you in gym class, and she says she could use your height.

"Just try out and see what happens," she says.

At the tryouts two girls you recognize from your physics class smile at you.

"There are two spots left on Varsity," the one named Deb says, dribbling up and passing you the ball, which you toss up into the hoop like you've done a million times in your own driveway. It drops in over the rim.

"Wow, that took me about a hundred tries," the other girl exclaims.

The three of you practice together, passing and dribbling and shooting, and then Coach Crowe mixes you up with the juniors and seniors who played on the team last year. After an hour of running up and down the floor, she tells everyone what a great job they did and sends you all off to catch the late bus.

"I hope you'll be back again tomorrow, May," she smiles at you.

"I will," you promise. Every part of your body smiles back at her.

"How tall are you, anyway?"

You shrug.

Who knows how tall you are?

Only that you are taller than Mother.

"Well, we'll see tomorrow," she waves you back into the locker room, with the others.

Deb guesses that you are close to six feet tall, at least an inch taller than she is. She sits next to you on the late bus and tells you all about how tryouts work and that they will last three days and then whoever makes the team will be posted on Friday. It's the same for the boys' team, because her brother played on the Varsity last year.

That night at dinner, you say, "I'm trying out for the girls' basketball team."

Helen finishes chewing a piece of well-done roast and with the meat still in her mouth says, "Is that where you were after school?"

You nod.

"Good for you, May." Dad moves James' sippy cup so it won't spill and set Mother off. He used to play basketball and he likes that you practice on the hoop he put up outside for Jacob.

Helen rolls her eyes. "Now, all you're going to talk about is basketball, I know it."

In one long two-year-old's garble, baby James repeats Helen's words and everyone laughs. Except Mother.

"You didn't get home until almost six."

Across the table, she stabs at the meat on her plate. Why is she so mad? "I took the late bus," you explain.

"Yeah, and if you make the team you'll be home late every night." Helen whines. Mother refuses to meet your eyes.

"Good for you, May." Dad reaches over, pulling a strip of fat off of the roast and putting it on his plate.

"Fine, eat more fat, give yourself a heart attack and leave me with all these damn kids," Mother says to him.

"Relax." Dad puts up his hand to calm her.

Mother turns toward you, her voice jumping up an octave, "There are enough activities here at home to keep both of these girls plenty busy."

"Let her be." Dad gives Mother a warning look and wipes the grease from his lips.

The piece of meat you are chewing tastes like leather.

"NO!" Mother slams her fork down on the table and hisses, "She damn-well better help out around here."

"She helps out plenty."

"She doesn't lift a finger."

You say nothing, just look at your plate and keep chewing. Dad used to be afraid of Mother when she went crazy like this. Now, he hardly seems to notice.

"That's enough," he says with a tired voice.

Mother jumps up.

"NO! I've had it with all of you."

Tears pour down her cheeks and her hands clutch together like they are hurting. "I'm so goddamn sick of you all."

Dad goes to her and she cries against his chest, "I work my fingers to the bone and these ungrateful little wretches… won't even…."

"Okay, let's just calm down here."

When baby James sees Mother crying, he starts to cry, too, and trying to wiggle down out of his booster seat, he reaches for Mother but she hollers, "Just get away from me. All of you! Just leave me alone," but Dad won't let her go, and she pounds her fists against his chest and he throws his arms around her to calm her down, but she screams louder and louder, until finally he lets go.

She runs to her room and you watch him chase after her. Helen starts to whimper.

Jacob and Gabe just keep eating.

James lets out a rare howl, so you grab his sippy cup, which was intentionally placed out of his reach, and offer it up to him. He stops crying, stares at it for a moment, then grabs it and puts it in his mouth, drinking ravenously.

Helen looks at you. "Why do you have to cause so much trouble. God... you're such a selfish bitch."

"Bitch... ha...." Gabe repeats, spitting reconstituted potatoes out onto his plate.

You get up, carry your plate to the sink, and turn on the hot water tap. Steam rises up and dampens your cheeks. Helen is trying to make you feel guilty. As the water warms your hands, you hear Mother and Dad arguing in their bedroom.

Mother says the word *pigsty* several times.

Something deep deep inside you knows you have to play basketball.

You turn the water up all the way.

The kitchen counters are a devastation of dishes and pots, pans and empty cans and crushed cereal boxes, things you usually put away when you come home after school.

"May." Helen comes up and shuts off the water. "What if she's pregnant again?" Her eyes look desperate, but now her voice is nice. "May, don't leave me with her."

You look at your sister. If you don't get to play basketball, some part of you will die.

"More sippy, May!" James shouts, swinging the sippy cup in circles above his head.

"Maybe I won't even make the team." You shrug, walk over and take the empty cup from James. Helen opens the refrigerator and hands you a jug of milk.

"You will," she says with resignation.

Gabe looks over at you and Helen. "Can I be done?"

Potatoes are smeared all over his face. He wants to go downstairs and watch TV, where he falls asleep every night.

Helen shakes her head and sighs. "Whatever." Then she mumbles, "I'm not your f'in mother."

Gabe laughs, gets up, and runs downstairs.

"I'll put James down if you do the dishes," you say to Helen.

"May, did you hear what I said?"

You refill the sippy cup, without responding. Another baby? You hope it's not true. You can't even think about it. "What makes you think that?" You ask, wiping the slime off the handle of James' cup before you give it back to him.

"I had to take care of the boys after school. She went to the doctor."

"Maybe it was for something else."

"She came home crying."

"I thought she couldn't have any more?" Remembering how she had to stay in the hospital after James."

"Yeah, but I think it was a Catholic thing, there was some kind of mix up and the doctor didn't tie her tubes, afterall. He told her to use birth control."

"Are you sure?"

Helen nods. "Please, don't leave me alone."

You look at Helen. She is standing next to the refrigerator. You hand her the milk jug. "I have to." You say softly, like somehow that will help.

It doesn't.

"May, more sippy!" James holds his empty cup up once more. He's sucked down the entire thing.

Helen stands there holding the milk jug. Her face goes pale. "She'll be so pissed. She'll take it out on me."

"More. More. More sippy!" James shouts.

You meet Helen's gaze. It's the least you can do. Her face is ghostly. "I have to try," you say again.

"No, you don't, but you'll . . ." Her voice fades away.

James starts to bang his cup on the table.

Both of you turn to look at James because neither one of you knows what to say next.

Finally, you turn around and grab the sippy cup. "No way, Jose.'" You unbuckle James and lift him down. He weighs a ton. Taking his chubby hand in yours, you lead him past Helen down the hall.

"Not tired, more sippy, please," James begs when he realizes where you are taking him.

You feel Helen's eyes on your back.

The refrigerator door opens and slams shut.

As you lead James into his room, you know it doesn't matter if Mother is or is not pregnant. It doesn't matter, because Helen is right about one thing, you will make the team. You will leave her behind, and a part of her will never catch up, because a part of her has already died.

CHAPTER 31

The Clothes Chute

THE NEXT day after school the late bus has adjusted its route and you get dropped off first instead of last. As you step off the bus, the bus driver asks, "You're May O'Malley, right?"

You nod up at him.

He smiles, "Good," he reaches for the door lever, "Let me know if this route change helps."

You nod. Not understanding.

Then the door closes and the bus gasps as he drives off.

When you walk through the front door you sense something is wrong. Mother is sitting at the kitchen table smoking a cigarette and sipping a Pepsi.

"Where's Gabe and James?"

Taking a long draw from her cigarette, she continues to stare out the window.

You listen carefully.

"Where's Helen and Jacob?" You try to keep a feeling of panic out of your voice.

Mother glances up at you, like she is surprised to see you, "Oh, May, it's you. You're home early?" she says this as if it is some kind of miracle. "I sent them off to take James for a walk. I couldn't stand another minute of their racket."

A little relieved and a little uneasy, you go to the refrigerator and pull an apple from the bin.

"Fine, ruin your dinner," Mother laughs, with what Helen calls her "Dr. Jekyll and Mrs. Hyde" laugh. "Why should I care, you kids'll be making your own dinner. None of you appreciate anything, anyway. And you, May, you may think you've won the battle with this sneaky after-school escapade of yours, but believe me, you have not won the war." She pauses and takes another drag of the cigarette.

You hear the hum from the television in the basement.

"Is Gabe downstairs?" you ask, as it suddenly occurs to you she didn't mention him.

She looks over at you, and her eyes have that far away look and she starts to laugh, again. The bite of apple becomes a sourball and you swallow it whole without even chewing.

"You'd better check the clothes chute."

Thoughts in your head begin to back up like a train.

You stare at her.

What has she done?

A word begins spelling itself backwards, over and over again, in your brain...

l-i-v-e-l-i-v-e-l-i-v-e-l-i-v-e

Mother snubs out her cigarette. At the same time, your body snaps into action and you turn and race down the stairs, past the blaring television set to the laundry room, where you find Gabe lying in a pile of dirty clothes.

Mother had locked him in the clothes chute.

His eyes are closed. The basement window throws shadowy slots of light across his face.

"Gabe? Gabe?" you choke as you unlock the latch. "Gabe?" For a split second your stomach wretches up into your throat.

He opens his eyes and struggles to sit up and look around.

You push the dirty clothes out of the way and try to help him out, but he resists.

"NO!" he cries.

"Gabe, it's okay."

"Ha… teach you a lesson," he says, and pushes past you, sliding down onto a table strewn with dirty clothes and then onto the floor.

"Ha… sorry you were born," he laughs running up the steps.

Then you hear Mother say in a sing-song voice, "There's my silly boy."

You lean your head against the wooden slats of the clothes chute because your heart is drumming so loudly you feel lightheaded. Several minutes pass and then, as if someone put you on automatic pilot, you walk over to a pile of clean clothes and begin to fold them and stack them in alphabetically ordered piles on the laundry table.

For some reason with each piece of clothing, you spell the owner's name backwards.

You just finish putting a pair of socks on *r-e-h-t-o-m*'s pile when Helen calls you up for dinner.

CHAPTER 32

The Favorite

YOU MAKE the team, and Mother and Dad have one final huge, screaming, swearing, door-kicking fight about you playing basketball. After Mother pitches a knife at Dad's head and it sticks sideways in the new walnut cabinet, Dad sends all of the kids to their rooms, including you. The screaming goes on until Mother finally retreats to her room in tears, and Dad comes down the hall to inform everyone they are free to move about safely again.

The boys immediately run downstairs to watch television.

Dad pops his head into your bedroom.

Helen is lying on her bed paging through a Seventeen magazine and you are sitting on the edge of yours holding a laundry basket filled with clean socks.

"May, we're going to let you play basketball. But promise me you will come directly home after practice and help as much as you can, okay?"

"I promise," you say quickly.

"Yeah, right, hurry home, May," Helen says under her breath.

Defensively, you hold up a sock. "I help out when I'm home."

"Yeah, but you're *never* home."

Dad says to Helen, "Now, don't you start in," then he looks at his watch. "I have a meeting tonight and Mother's not feeling well. You two will have to put your brothers to bed."

"What's new?" Helen whispers resentfully.

Dad starts to close the door but on second thought opens it again and looks at Helen. "And don't you be talking on the phone all night. Your Mother told me last night you were on there for over an hour. Who were you talking to?"

Helen turns a page roughly.

"Helen?"

Helen sighs and looks up at him.

"What—already?"

"You heard what I said."

"A friend, okay," she says, and looks back down at the magazine. He glances at his watch again. "Well, just remember family comes before friends. And no dates until you're sixteen." Distractedly, he closes the door.

"Fuck off," Helen says so quietly only you hear.

After the garage door opens and closes, Helen slams her magazine shut, lies back on her pillow, and closes her eyes. "God, I hate this family."

You don't like it when Helen talks like this. But if you say anything she'll cry, so you hold up a pair of candy-striped toe socks.

"Are these yours?"

She opens her eyes.

The socks are really yours, a Secret Santa gift from the girls' basketball team Christmas gift exchange, but Helen doesn't know that, so you ball them up and toss them onto her bed.

Helen picks the socks up and unfurls them with a snap of her wrist.

She holds them up and fingers the little multicolored knit toes and laughs. "Oh my God, where did these come from? They are absolutely hideous."

Your eyes meet hers. She looks so sad it's almost hard to hold her gaze, but you do, because you feel bad about leaving her with everything, just not bad enough to quit the basketball team.

"I thought they were yours," you smile, pretending to be serious.

"Yeah, right." She balls them back up and tosses them at you.

You pull off the socks you're wearing and put on the toe socks and jump up onto the bed and begin to disco dance like they do on Soul Train.

Helen starts to laugh.

You leap from bed to bed and dance around her, making your toes wiggle with the imaginary music and picking up loose socks with the toes of the toe socks and flinging them at her.

She screeches with laughter.

Then a holey pair of Jacob's sweat socks land on her face and she flings them back at you.

"They're clean," you say, rubbing them against your own face and flinging them back at her and suddenly socks are flying all over the room, and Helen is laughing so hard she falls off her bed and lies between your beds, panting.

You keep laughing and dancing and flinging socks. But Helen curls up in a ball between the two beds, her laughter turning to sobs, which takes you a moment to register. You lean over the edge of your bed.

"Helen?

You want to put your hand on her shoulder. But you're sure it will upset her more.

"Next year you can play basketball, too," you say.

"Yeah, right, and who will take care of the boys?" She drops her hands and looks at you angrily. Her face is blotchy and red. "She already said I'd better not pull the same stunt as you. See?" She sits up and kneels at your feet and pulls up the sleeve of her shirt. At first you only see the red welt on the back of her arm, but when you look closer you see teeth marks. There is no way in hell Helen could have bit herself there.

"See!" she sniffles. "Because I didn't want to take care of James."

Your own arm starts to ache.

"I hate this family." Helen flops herself back up onto her bed.

You have a sick feeling in your stomach.

"You know what she did to Gabe today?"

You nod. No words come out.

"You do?"

You nod again.

"No you don't. You weren't even here and it's your fault, why can't you just come home after school? Then she wouldn't be such a psycho!"

One by one you pick up the socks that landed on your bed and begin tossing them back into the basket.

Helen sits up and wipes her eyes with a stray white sock. Then she starts throwing the stray socks on her side of the room in the general direction of the basket.

"Jerome says this whole family is fucked up and she should go to jail."

"Who's Jerome?"

"A friend."

"Your boyfriend?"

"Not really, just a friend, okay?"

"What did you tell him?" you say, incredulous.

"Nothing."

You stop collecting socks and stare at her. She lies back down on her bed and closes her eyes.

"You did too."

"No I didn't."

"Then why'd he say she should go to jail?"

"Because his mom used to work for social services."

"What's that?"

Helen opens her eyes. "I can't believe how stupid you are," she sighs.

She rolls her eyes dramatically. "It's like plainclothes police. They make sure people aren't beating the crap out of their kids."

You start to say, "She only…." But you stop, the bite mark fresh in your mind.

"Yeah, you don't know, it's different for you because you're Dad's favorite."

Dropping another sock in the basket, you sit down on the edge of your bed. Your head begins to throb. Helen's right, Mother doesn't come at you much at night, anymore, and when she does, she's aiming for Helen or Jacob or Gabe. Not you. In fact, she steers clear of you. The strange thing is, you would rather she come after you, because you hate the sound of crying.

What Helen doesn't know is that you would rather be dead than listen to someone cry, because every time you hear crying, it reminds you of Hal and it makes your head hurt.

Thinking about Mother going to jail makes your heart want to run like a rabbit. Then you think *she might die,* and it would be your fault. If she is pregnant, *the baby might die too.*

Helen imitates Mother's fake sing-song voice. "Oh, no, May must play basketball, she can't help out. Oh, no, May has homework, she can't lift a finger. Oh, no, May is the favo—"

You jump to your feet and try to stuff a sock in her mouth. "Shut up!"

"Stay away from me… owwww!"

You thump her hard on the back.

Socks, curses, and karate kicks start flying. Helen's heel hits you square on the nose. Blood gushing, you retreat to the bathroom, cupping your hands to catch the blood.

When you finally get back, Helen's fallen asleep with her face pressed into the magazine, the bedside lamp still on, and her bare legs sticking out under her nightgown. You sit on the edge of your bed pressing the matchbook under your nose. Though you are mad, you watch Helen while she sleeps. Even in her sleep, she looks sad. You wish she could play basketball, too, but she's right. She is not Dad's favorite. You are. Someone has to stay home to help Mother. It's just the way it is.

CHAPTER 33

The Friend

IN THE months that follow, you see no signs that your mother is prenant again. Still, you try to help, and it doesn't make her hate you or anyone else any less.

You hope Helen is not right. You have suspicions that she may have told you this to keep you from playing basketball, but it is equally likely that Mother made Helen think this so Helen would tell you, and then you'd feel so guilty you'd come home every night after school instead of playing basketball.

Helen has started sneaking out the window in the middle of the night. She knows you won't tell on her, and if you ask where she's going, she just says, "Out."

Mother continues to complain. So Dad decides to buy a new car, a Corvette, and he gives you the Cadillac so you can help even more. "Come right home after practice, May," he says, tossing the keys on his way out the door. "We all have to do our part."

Helen tries to make you her personal chauffer.

"Can you drop me and Jacob at Pizza Hut?" She comes bounding down the basement steps while you're ironing Dad's shirts.

"I have to get Gabe at seven."

"It's near there."

"It is not."

She keeps begging. "Since when do you and Jacob hang out together on a Saturday night?" You smooth out the shirt in your hand.

"Since the skating rink opened."

You've heard about the skating rink, but you've never been there.

"Jerome's meeting us, then we're going skating. It's bring-your-brother-for-free night." Helen opens the dryer and begins to fold clothes that tumble out. Suddenly, you feel left out.

"Can I bring Gabe?"

"He's too little," Helen slices her arm across her waist. "There's a chart on the wall, no one this short can get in."

You sense she's lying. But why?

"Please, May, just this once."

"You said Jerome has a car, why can't he pick you up, like he does in the middle of the night?"

Helen adds a white shirt to your pile. "May..." she doesn't finish.

You spray a mixture of starch and water on the white shirt.

She sighs. "Okay, okay, you'll see when you drop us off."

Less than a half-hour later, pulling up next to the ancient Lincoln Town car, you say, "That's Jerome's car?"

There are fringe balls lining the back window and two black fuzzy dice hang from the rearview mirror. The car has no back bumper and the license plate is duct-taped to the back trunk.

"Yeah," Helen says, "He's not snotty and what's best of all," she pauses, as if waiting for some kind of drum roll, "he lives in our old house."

You stare at the fuzzy dice. The car is empty. "In Pig Valley?" you ask.

Jacob, who hasn't said a word for weeks, whispers from the back seat, "Cool, a ghetto cruiser."

"He must have gone in," Helen says, opening her car door. She gets out, smiles, and looks back at Jacob, "Don't embarrass me, okay?" she says, before slamming the car door.

You turn and look at Jacob. He shrugs and jumps out to join her.

"Just make sure you really go skating," you say after him.

He closes the car door acting like he doesn't hear.

He's taller than Helen, even though he's still in junior high.

The next morning, Dad has already left early when Helen comes tearing into the bathroom.

"MAKE HER STOP! PLEASE MAY, TELL HER, WE ONLY WENT SKATING!" She rushes behind you.

"PLEASE MAY!"

Mother appears in the bathroom doorway, holding a metal spoon above her head. "You little whore! You'll tell me where you were last night or I'll beat it out of you."

Behind you, Helen cowers. Mother can't get to her unless she deals with you first.

"Get out of my way!"

You don't budge.

Mother aims for your face, but your well-honed basketball reflexes kick in and you drop your toothbrush and raise your arm managing to block the blow, but the metal slices into the skin of your arm and you grab her wrist and squeeze it. Hard. So hard it feels like it could snap off in your hand. You swallow the toothpaste frothing in your mouth, and stand above her, blood dripping onto the gray and pink tile floor. Helen is whimpering behind you, and you say slowly, in a voice that bubbles up from somewhere deep, "Don't ever hit me again."

"Let me go, you little she-devil," Mother says, trying to shake you loose.

You hold tight.

"Dad told you not to hit anymore."

"She has it coming. Whoring around in the middle of the night."

She tries to push past you, and you twist her wrist so hard she is forced to back up.

She laughs. "You think your Father gives a damn about any of you?"

Behind you, Helen begins to howl.

You wish she would stop crying but instead she gets louder and louder. And Mother begins to rant. "That's right, she knows, he doesn't give a damn if any of us are dead or alive. As long as he can gallop off to his little play-pen all day."

Her spit lands on your face and when you blink she tries to reach around you with her other arm and grab Helen's hair, but you are too quick for her, and you crank down on her wrist and back her out of the bathroom.

"And *you*, with your little disappearing act, you've got him fooled, but you don't fool me, and believe me, you'll be sorry y—"

Her free hand shoots up for your hair but you grab it and you hear the same deep voice come out of you, a voice you hardly recognize. Calmly, deliberately, it says, "I'll call the police."

And you see fear flash across her eyes and her arms suddenly go limp, and releasing her wrists you push her away and she squints at you and starts to laugh. A fake laugh.

"They'll never believe you, May. Never." She turns and heads back down the hall, cursing and laughing.

After you hear the kitchen drawer open and the spoon being shoved back in the drawer and the drawer closing again, you turn around. Helen is on her knees rocking and covering her ears.

"Shush, Helen."

You help her to her feet but she won't even look at you. She staggers past you like a zombie.

You get a washcloth out of the linen closet and start sopping up the blood on the floor but the cut is so deep blood just gushes out and there are no band-aids in the linen closet, so you go and find one of Jacob's white tube socks and tie it around your elbow, tourniquet-style. And then you go back to the bathroom. You decide to clean the whole thing and get out the Comet cleanser and the scrub bucket and you wash the tub, the shower, the toilet, everything from top to bottom.

Until it sparkles.

When you are finally finished, you feel good, surprisingly good. But you can't stop hearing Mother's words: *They'll never believe you.*

CHAPTER 34

The Truth

MOTHER'S DOOR is locked.

Downstairs Saturday morning cartoons are blasting out of the television set where all three of the boys are camped out. In the kitchen you dig around in the cabinet for bread, but all you can find are two stale ends left in a plastic bag and you swear at Jacob under your breath because you know he probably pigged it up, making cinnamon toast for breakfast.

You hear Helen laughing back in your bedroom. You hope it is Jerome on the phone and that he's helping her emerge from her zombie state, but when you get back to the room, Helen is not on the phone, she's sitting on the edge of her bed staring at you.

"What are you doing?" you ask.

Something is odd about the way she looks.

She sniffles and wipes at her nose with the sleeve of her shirt and then laughs again. "I told him."

"Who?" You point to a line of fine white powder just below her nose. "You have baby powder on your lip."

She wipes at it and laughs, "I told Dad."

"You told Dad what?"

"She did it. Now, she's going to do it to me."

"What?" you ask cautiously.

"Shut me up once and for all."

Your stomach flip flops.

"It was her. I heard. I was under the bed. I heard."

"What was her?"

You stare at Helen's blue eyes. Her pupils are dilated and you wonder if the crying made them look like this.

"What did she say?" you ask cautiously.

"She said she was going to shut me up once and for all. And that's when I remembered,

May. It wasn't Mr. Novak's car. It was her."

Your stomach begins doing flip-flops.

"What was her?"

"H-a-l." She spells it.

She is talking about the one thing no one in your family ever talks about.

"What's the matter with your eyes?" you ask.

She starts to laugh. She sniffles and wipes at her nose again. "She's the liar."

A car honks out in the driveway and you go look out the window and see Jerome.

"Are you crazy? You shouldn't have him come here." You watch the car slow down in front of the house and turn into the driveway.

Helen laughs. "Dad's gone as usual."

You've heard rumors at school that Jerome is a drug dealer and he's just using Helen to get to the rich white kids. But in this moment, all you can think of is missing basketball practice."Who's going to watch the boys?" you say in a panic.

Picking up her purse Helen smiles coyly. "Ask me if I care." She starts running down the hall heading for the front door.

You chase after her.

"Helen, wait… what about the boys?"

At the front door, she spins around and points in the direction of Mother's bedroom with such intensity that you freeze in your tracks. "He wouldn't stop crying, just like me, so she slammed his head, she slammed it, May. It wasn't Mr. Novak's fault. Dad remembers. Seven trillion scotch and waters won't block it out." Helen catches her breath. Then her voice gets low and scary. "She's the god-damn lying whore in this family. Not me."

You stare at Helen.

She laughs.

"Don't bother waiting up for me, Sis, I might not be home until late, really, really late. Maybe never." She laughs again.

The door slams shut.

Through the front picture window you watch Jerome's ghetto cruiser drive off down the wide paved road. You sink down on the blue velvet chair in the living room. The *Scooby Doo* theme song drifts up through the basement door.

You wish you could remember.

But you don't, you can't even remember what Hal looked like anymore, so you force yourself up because Gabe has come running up to report that Jacob spilled Cheerios on the rug and James wiped it up with his pajama bottoms and now he can't find clean underwear and he's running around naked in the basement and there isn't time to think about this anymore, basketball practice starts in 20 minutes, and now you must dress the boys and take them with you.

"Helen left with Jerome and I've got practice, so do you want to stay here with the boys or do you want me to drop you at playland and pick you up after?" you say to Jacob as you snap off the television set.

"Hey!" Jacob cries.

"Ha! Playland. Say Playland, Jacob." Gabe runs around in circles.

Jacob rousts himself from the sofa. His hair is greasy and he looks tired and hung over.

"I'll give you some of the grocery money to use for lunch," you offer.

Jacob pulls a huge wad of cash from his pocket. "Don't need it."

The wad is rolled up and tied in a rubber band. It looks like a lot of money.

"Helen paid me off not to narc on her and Jerome."

"Great," you say.

"It's cool, May. I'll buy the guys lunch, just don't leave me here."

You've become accustomed to being in charge, to giving orders. And Jacob, for the most part, has become accustomed to obeying. He catches the keys when you toss them and takes Gabe's hand and trudges toward the garage.

"Ha! Playland, playland, playland," Gabe repeats on each step.

In the laundry room, you help James dress himself in clean clothes. He wears Gabe's old trainer underwear, and it bunches up under his pants, which are way too tight. Those were Gabe's, too, and the combination makes him look like he's still wearing diapers, but it doesn't seem to bother him. Especially after you promise to read him Winnie the Pooh later, if he hurries.

You hear the garage door open and the car start and the radio blast on.

Jacob has started the car.

You pull James' jacket on and take him out to the garage, "Buckle him in," you order Jacob, who is sitting in the driver's seat pretending to be like Speed Racer, which makes Gabe laugh and holler over the noise on the radio, "GO FASTER!"

You reach across and turn down the sound and head back into the house for your basketball shoes. The radio cranks back up full blast.

It's *Stairway to Heaven.* Jacob loves Led Zeppelin.

You race back down the hall to your room and dig your gym bag out of the closet. Helen has piled her dirty clothes on top, and out of a pair of jeans drops a gold compact, which spills open. It's not makeup.

Inside is a hollow gold tube, the size of a stubby miniature golf pencil, and an empty white packet with the words

SNOW SEAL stamped on it. So it wasn't baby powder dusted on Helen's lip, and Helen is getting herself into something bad, but the car honks out in the garage where the boys are waiting. A sound is coming from Mother's room, and you drop the gym bag and go to her door to listen.

Moaning and crying. A wounded animal sound.

"Mother?" you call softly.

You try the door but it's locked.

"Mother?" you say again, this time a little louder.

The moaning sound stops. It gets quiet.

"Mother?"

"Just go, please go," she whispers hoarsely from the other side.

At the garage door you hear the shower water turn on and in your mind's eye you see her curled up in a ball on the shower floor naked, breasts shrunken, clutching herself and rocking with the shower water spraying down. Her skin is scraped and raw from the tile floor. You can see her pressing her feet against the wall trying to stop herself from crying, but the sounds just keep coming out and you can feel her heart pounding and the rush of blood in her ears.

She moans. "Please, May, just leave me alone. Just go."

Jacob opens the garage door, "Are you coming?"

The sound of Led Zeppelin blasts into the hallway, *"And she's buying a stairway to heaaaaav...."*

Everything in you wants to stay, to help.

The horn of the car starts to honk.

"Gabe, knock it off," Jacob screams through the open garage door. Then he hears Mother. "What the hell?"

"She wants us to leave her alone."

You both stand there listening. The car starts to honk again.

"Gabe!" Jacob turns toward the garage and you follow him closing the door behind you.

A block away from the house, before Jacob's favorite song finishes, you switch off the radio and pull to the side of the road.

"That's the best part!" Jacob protests.

You put your head in your hands. "I have to think."

His hand flies for the knob again and inside of you something explodes. You feel yourself lunge across the seat and you grab him by the throat and start screaming, "I told you I have to think!"

Jacob doesn't fight back, he lets his body go limp and this makes you want to shake him harder. You pound on him with your fist and he curls down in the seat but still doesn't fight back. This makes you madder. And you pound harder until he yells, "Quit being like MOM!" and your fist freezes in mid-air, and you stop, and blink, and now you feel your own heart taking over your entire body with its beating and for a split second you forget who you are and Jacob reaches over to the radio knob cutting the sound just as the last line of the song fills up the car "*she's buying a stairway to h e a v e n....*"

"Ha! Hal's in Heaven," Gabe yells from the back seat.

"Why don't you make *him* shut up, May! Why don't you go back there and hurt *him*, huh?" Jacob rubs his hand against a red line on his neck as you pull back.

"Please… I'm not really like her, am I?" you say, and Jacob refuses to look at you and for a split second it is silent inside of the car.

"Ha! Hal's an angel." Gabe pokes his feet against Jacob's seat.

Jacob spins around but you put your hand on his arm. He looks at you, pauses, and says, "He's not supposed to talk about Hal! He wasn't even fucking alive! He didn't even know Hal. So if you're going to shut anyone up, why don't you shut him up?"

"Ha. Hal's in heaven. He's an angel now. We're not supposed to talk about it!" Gabe yells from the back seat.

You turn around. "Please Gabe, let's talk about it later, okay?"

"Ha. Thing one and thing two don't know what to do…" he says, lowering his voice pointing to the Dr. Suess book laying on the back seat. You reach back and hand it to him.

"Helen is more like her than you are," Jacob says as you turn back around. His once-bright eyes look dull and tired, but he smiles, "You're aren't that bad—yet."

And when Jacob says Helen's name, you know what you need to do.

You are the oldest.

When you drive right past McDonalds Gabe shouts, "Ha! Missed it!"

"I thought you had practice, where are you taking us?" Jacob asks.

"Pig Valley," you say.

CHAPTER 35

The Old House

"WHY?" JACOB tries to turn the radio up a little and
you give him a look until he turns it back down.

"Because it needs to be *all* of us."

"May, what the hell are you talking about?"

"Shush," you say, steering the Cadillac off of the freeway
ramp onto Point Road. As Pig Valley unfolds before you,
you see how much has changed. Houses are boarded up
and the once-tidy lawns are strewn with empty beer bottles, food wrappers, old tires, and a menagerie of garbage.
Locker's Flower House has become a body shop, and a col-
lection of smashed-up cars waits in the parking lot to be
worked on. The brewery is still there but they've added razor
wire to the chain link fence and an automated wrought iron
security gate lets the semis in and out. A teenager wearing
baggy jeans that hang half way off his butt and a hat that is
cocked sideways on his head is swinging around, snapping
his fingers like he's in his own little world.

247

"Phew," Jacob says. "This place sure has changed." He rolls down his window, "It still smells the same, though."

And even though your nose doesn't work as well as it used to, you can smell the hides from the tannery and the yeast and the malt from the brewery and just a hint of chocolate in the air.

"It does," you agree, and you pull the car up in front of your old house. The blue paint is peeling. The front porch railing has rotted and fallen off. Someone has parked a Harley in the driveway and the Novak's old side-by-side next door is in worse shape. Stones have fallen off the chimney and someone has installed iron bars on the first floor windows that have left rusty streaks down the dirty white siding.

"May, how do you know Helen is even here?"

You point. Parked way back in the driveway you see Jerome's car.

Jacob turns to look. "*He* lives here?"

You nod and glance in the back seat. Their heads tilted together, Gabe and James are fast asleep.

"Hang with them," you whisper to Jacob.

"Where are you going?"

"To find Helen."

"She won't come home anyway." Jacob studies the front door.

"We're not going home."

Jacob laughs, "Fine by me."

He thinks you are joking.

"I'll be right back," you say, and get out and shut the car door quietly.

CHAPTER 36

The Same Kid

YOU LOOK both ways and make a dash across Point Road. You climb the steps. The wire from the doorbell is hanging off the siding, but you press it anyway. A faint buzz tells you it works.

It looks dark inside. You wonder what in the world brought Helen back here and how she got hooked up with Jerome. It feels strange to be back in Pig Valley. You press again, and wait.

"Please, Helen, be here," you whisper.

You ring one more time.

Finally, you give up and go back to the car, but the windows are cracked, the doors locked, Gabe and James are still sound asleep, and Jacob is nowhere to be found. Then you hear Jacob, "May, they're back here." And you see Helen is sitting on the grass, her knees pulled up to her chin, her fingers in her ears, and her head tucked down like she's hiding.

Jerome is leaning over her, trying to talk to her.

He looks up and stares at you. You run up, glaring back at him. You're too angry to be afraid.

"Helen? Helen? Are you okay?"

Jerome takes a step back. "She came on her own. I didn't do anything. She ain't well," he says.

"I know what's wrong with her," you fire back at him. "I know what you gave her."

Jerome holds his hands up. "She was supposed to just hand it over. I told her not to."

You ignore him and lean down next to Helen.

"Come on," you say softly.

"This is where they found him," she says. She is pointing to the cracked cement driveway. And you realize where you are… you are standing on the spot where the Novak's driveway used to be, the spot where they found Hal's body, and six months later, Mr. Novak's. And you look up, expecting to see the white picket fence, the rows of tomato plants, the red, white, and purple petunias you once helped plant.

Jacob brushes his hair from his eyes.

"How come I can't remember?" he says.

"You will, Jacob," Helen says, "Some day, you will."

"Helen, come on." You take her gently by the shoulders and try to help her up, but she shakes her head. "You guys go home."

"We're not going home," you say.

"Then where, May?" Jacob looks at you, his forehead furrows.

"California."

"California?" Jacob rolls his eyes. "Yeah, right."

Helen looks at you for the first time. "Seriously?" she says, and your eyes meet and you see that she is coming back into herself.

"Seriously," you say.

Jacob grabs her other arm and both of you help her to her feet. "Okay then, California. Aunt Cleo here we come. That's cool."

Helen wipes her eyes. "I was gonna go on my own."

"I know."

Helen smiles a little. "Yeah, I figured."

"Gabe and James, too?" Jacob asks.

"Oh my God, they're with you?" Helen says. The color is beginning to come back into her face but she is unsteady on her feet.

"All of us," you say.

Helen looks down. "Except Hal." She glances back at Jerome.

Jerome looks at you, "I was only tryin' to help with the money part," he says.

You believe him.

Suddenly you remember his face and why he looks so familiar. You know him—from that day your Dad told you to stay in the car, and you stepped out into that beat-to-hell neighborhood and that boy wearing Kareem Abdul Jabbar's jersey stepped out onto the porch and he asked you, "What you doin' here?"

This was him—the same kid.

A strange shiver rolls down your spine, like somehow you've both been here before, you both know each other, even though you really don't, but how did he end up living in your old house? How did Helen hook up with him? Was this where she came when she snuck out the window at night, this spot, where Hal died?

CHAPTER 37

The Light

A CAR horn honks. You look back and see Gabe is pressing his face against the window watching all of you.

Jacob sighs. "You got anything to tranquilize Gabe with?"

"Jacob!" You say with a big sister voice.

Jacob holds up his hand, "Just kidding, don't blow another gasket, May."

"What about gas and food and all that?" Helen says looking at you.

Her legs wobble. You and Jacob simultaneously steady her as she keeps talking. "May, do you know how far California is? We can't just take off, we'll need money and clothes and stuff and I don't have my license yet."

Jacob and Jerome reach into their respective pockets and each pulls out a wad of cash. Jerome hands his wad to Jacob, who holds the money up in the air and laughs. "Got it covered."

"You'll need to help May drive," Helen tells Jerome.

"Girrrl, you won't make it past the state line with me behind that wheel." Jerome looks at the red Cadillac, then snaps his fingers, "I got an idea," he says and races off down the block.

You and Helen and Jacob watch him run into the body shop in Locker's old flower shop. He brings out an older gray-haired man and points to the red Cadillac. All three of you know what he's up to. Jacob runs his thumb through the pile of cash in his hand, "He better go for something basic, no Corvettes."

"What if Dad comes after us?" Helen says quietly.

"What if he doesn't?" you say just as quietly back.

"Will we make it, May? What if we really do, what if we really get all the way out there by ourselves and Aunt Cleo sends us back?"

Helen puts her hand on your arm and turns you toward her.

Your eyes meet.

You sense her desperation. Her sadness. The kind of sadness you saw years ago in the eyes of the lonely lowland gorilla at the public zoo. Sampson. Sitting in that cage for years and years and years. People said he was still alive, but you doubted he'd ever really lived, and you think of Hal, and how many ways there are to die.

"May, tell me."

In Helen's voice you hear Mother's howl.

"Will we, May?" She is about to start cryng again.

You close your eyes, because now you've learned to go into time pockets at will. You listen to Helen and Jacob breathing. Then, in your head you say Hal's name and the colors come in a rush of spiral light and you see Aunt Cleo sitting on the edge of a sailboat pointing out into the water, and all of you are there, though you are older, taller, thinner and tan. Jacob looks almost like a man, Gabe is wearing glasses, James is holding a telescope and everyone is looking at the water. Just behind Helen, whose hair is so long it hangs down to her waist, you see fins breaking the surface and you wonder if they are sharks or dolphins, but you don't have to wonder long because your eyes pop open—you know.

You take Helen by the shoulders and look directly into her eyes and you say, "She'll believe us, Helen. She will."

Helen cries anyway. She is not sure if she believes you.

Jerome pulls up in an old brown Ford station wagon. He rolls down the window. "Okay, you'd better collect those other two and hit the road." He points at the red Cadillac where Gabe still has his nose pressed against the glass, and just to make sure that all of you know he has been listening, Gabe puts his mouth up to the opening at the top of the window and hollers at the top of his lungs, "Ha!"

You and Helen and Jacob start laughing.

Jerome jumps out of the idling car. "Maybe that one you should tie on top."

"Excellent idea," Jacob agrees and with Jerome's help he starts to transfer Gabe and James and their car seats to the new car.

"Better go, big sis boss, you got a long drive and the light is fading fast." Jerome looks over his shoulder at the western sky. The sun is starting to go down, there's an orange glow peeking around the brewery smokestacks. All the smells of Pig Valley surround you like an invisible shield.

The yeast. The chocolate. The tannery.

Jerome holds out Gabe's book, *The Cat in the Hat.* "It's settin' fast," he says.

"You know where you're goin'," he says.

It's not a question really. His eyes hold yours—just like they did that day years ago. You're both still a little afraid, but it feels different this time, and his words land in your brain like soft drops of rain.

You nod.

He smiles. "That's right sister, follow the light."

You take the book from his outstretched hand. You want to say more, to thank him but no words come, so you open the driver's door and get in.

Jerome hugs Helen and helps her into the front seat. "Go on, you'll be okay." He steps back and winks. "You know where to find me when you come back to visit. Dry up them tears."

Jacob has settled both the boys in the back of the Ford. James is still asleep, his chubby cheeks flushed red with the warmth in the car. Gabe is watching Jacob who smiles at you in the rearview mirror and flashes a thumbs up. "All set for go."

"Ha! All set for go." Gabe repeats, putting his thumbs up in the air too.

Helen wipes at her eyes and looks over at you. "Aunt Cleo better believe us, May. You'd better be right."

You take a deep breath because now you know what you know, and Helen will just have to trust you on this—everything is going to be okay.

Even Hal is okay, now.

CHAPTER 38

The New Beginning

"MAY, you'd better be sure."

"I am."

About the Author

BRIDGET BIRDSALL received her MFA in Writing for Children and Young Adults from Vermont College. In 2009, she was a finalist for A Room of Her Own's (AROHO's) $50,000 Gift Of Freedom Award. Her young adult novel *August Atlas,* which is currently seeking a publisher, received an honorable mention in the University of Wisconsin–Madison Writer's Institute First Page Contest. *Ordinary Angels* took first place. She resides in Madison, Wisconsin. Her visual art and her prize-winning short story *Miracle on Monkey Mountain* can be viewed at www.bridgetbirdsall.com.